A MIND FOR MYSTERIES

BY

ROBIN BRANDE

A Mind for Mysteries
5 Winnie Parsons Mysteries
By Robin Brande

Published by Ryer Publishing
www.ryerpublishing.com
Copyright 2025 by Robin Brande
www.robinbrande.com
Art by byemoke/Deposit Photos and
Mappingz, OmarLoveıart, and ftyaadha/Canva
Ebook ISBN: 978-1-952383-04-5
Paperback ISBN: 978-1-952383-29-8
Hardback ISBN: 978-1-952383-66-3

ALSO BY ROBIN BRANDE

<u>Winnie Parsons Mysteries</u>

A Mind for Mysteries (Collection)

The Genius Track

A Man of Appetites

A Drop of Sweat

The Long Gray Hook

The Slip of a Rib

The Cabin Ghost

The Secret Juror

The Truth Chamber

<u>Dove Season Universe</u>

Dove Season

Finder

Seeker

Believer

Maker

Explorer

Young Adult

Evolution, Me & Other Freaks of Nature

Fat Cat

Doggirl

Replay

Into the Parallel

Caught in the Parallel

Seize the Parallel

Beyond the Parallel

Book of Earth

Book of Water

Romance

Love Proof

Freefall

Heart of Ice

Fire and Ice

Self-Help

What If You're Doing It Right?

What If You're Doing It Right? For Teens

Collections

The Love of a Good Dog

Mountain Tough

The Miraculous Unknown

Life with the Afterlife

Heart of the Future

CONTENTS

INTRODUCTION

I have always loved any book I can get my hands on about ESP, psychic powers, clairvoyance, any of it.

Fiction, non-fiction, all of it. Give me, please.

But what I've always wanted to know is how someone with those powers lives his or her everyday life. What do you do when you can see, hear, and know what other people can't? Do you still bake cookies, walk your dog, go to Target? If so, how are those experiences *different*?

This collection of mysteries about retired psychology professor and clairvoyant Dr. Winifred Parsons is my exploration of that. I wanted to write a life that wasn't all flash and dazzle and jazz hands. For Winnie Parsons, her psi ability is just like any other talent someone might have. And she treats it the same way an athlete or musical genius might treat his or her own talent: by trying to get better at it all the time.

I hope you enjoy this collection as much as I loved writing every story in it. As you'll see, I also took the opportunity to weave in some of the cool frontier science I've researched over the years. Can't get enough of that, either.

Now let's go see what Winnie and her yellow Lab Clover are up to over the Thanksgiving holiday in THE GENIUS TRACK. Enjoy!

~Robin Brande

A MIND FOR MYSTERIES

THE GENIUS TRACK

1

Selena Martez scrunched down further into her crimson fleece hoodie and leaned against her mother while they waited for Dr. Parsons to answer the doorbell.

"It will be fine," her mother said. Although Selena could tell from her voice that she wasn't so sure, either. "If you don't like her, we won't stay."

Selena nodded. She felt tired again this morning. Exhausted to the bone. Yet her nerves were buzzing now like bees inside her blood. She clenched her teeth together and tried to force herself to stop shaking.

She wanted to be here, but she didn't. The whole thing sounded so weird.

But also, in a way, exciting.

If this were a TV show, she would watch it. But to be living it instead ...

Selena and her mother stood in front of a solid-looking wooden door set within a high stucco wall that surrounded Dr. Parsons's house. An old, branchy mesquite tree stretched tall and wide above them, shading the front entrance.

The houses in this neighborhood looked old, as old as some of the buildings at the University of Arizona a few blocks away. From what Selena's mother said, a lot of professors lived in the area since they could walk to work.

Besides the big mesquite tree, there were lots of pretty desert flowers clumped all around the front walkway: white oleanders, pink Mexican primrose, red and purple salvia. All of them still held their blooms this late in November.

Selena always liked this time of year best—or at least she used to. By Thanksgiving, the heat of Tucson's endless summer finally gave way to the desert's version of fall. She could dress in thick, fluffy clothes, wear thick wool socks around the house. It was like living somewhere north for a few months, just like Selena always dreamed of doing.

And her birthday was in November, which used to feel special, too. She was seventeen now. Finally a senior at Desert Wells High School. On track to apply to the best universities on both coasts—Stanford, CalTech, Princeton—along with her own hometown University of Arizona.

If she lived long enough to do it.

For the past month Selena had felt like a full-time science experiment rather than a student. What tests hadn't the doctors done? Blood work, brain scans, extensive neurological work-ups—while Selena had to work harder than ever to keep up with her classes.

A lot of seniors were over school by now. They felt like coasting. Taking as few classes as possible. Just getting through it so they could get on to college or work or whatever their dreams of adulting looked like.

Selena was taking a full load, plus.

It was the *plus* that had her the most worried. If she couldn't hack it in Mr. Spence's Genius Track, then she might as well kiss all those universities goodbye.

It was why she and her mother decided to come to Dr. Parsons. To try something different, something drastic.

When her mother first pressed the doorbell embedded in the stucco wall, Selena had heard a dog bark from somewhere inside the house.

Now the exterior wooden door opened, and she saw the dog before she noticed the woman.

Selena knelt down, not even bothering to ask if she could pet the gorgeous yellow Labrador. Selena and dogs always understood each other. The dog tilted her head, inviting Selena to scratch her behind the offered ear.

"What's your name?" Selena asked the dog, as if expecting the Lab to answer.

"This is Clover," Dr. Parsons said. "She always knows who she likes."

Selena glanced up from where she crouched. She pulled the hoodie back a little so she could see the woman standing behind the dog.

Dr. Parsons looked shorter than Selena, maybe only five-foot-three or four. She reminded Selena a little of her grandmother. Small, but sturdy. Not so skinny that you might be afraid of breaking her if you hugged too hard.

The doctor had wavy, chin-length, blondish-white hair that looked damp on the tips, as though she'd only just stepped out of the shower and toweled her hair dry.

She wore comfortable-looking, stretchy gray pants and a sky-blue T-shirt underneath an oversized green plaid flannel shirt.

From where she knelt in front of the Labrador, Selena could see the heels of Dr. Parsons's thick gray wool socks poking out of the back of her fleece-lined slide-in shoes. They might even be slippers, although

Dr. Parsons seemed too dignified to meet her guests at the door in anything other than formal shoes.

Dignified, but casual. Dr. Parsons wore no makeup. Her only jewelry was a plain gold wedding ring. She wore glasses with black plastic frames that made her look like the college professor she once was.

Behind the glasses Selena could see Dr. Parsons's calm green eyes gazing down at her, studying her. The doctor was obviously as curious about Selena as Selena was about her.

Dr. Parsons smiled, a genuine and friendly smile.

Selena looked away, suddenly feeling shy. She went back to petting Clover.

But she could feel the tightness in her shoulders and her chest start to loosen.

She let out a quiet breath. Her heart wasn't thumping quite so hard as it had on the drive over.

Maybe this would be all right. Maybe it would help.

They had only been with Dr. Parsons for a minute or two, but already something about the woman made Selena feel safe. Maybe it was her friendly dog, whose tongue was lolling out as she panted against Selena's cheek.

Or maybe it was because Dr. Parsons's smile seemed real. She didn't look as scary or as stern as some of the other doctors.

Selena already knew from her mother before they even came here that Dr. Parsons would be different.

That might be good ... or not.

"How are you both?" Dr. Parsons asked.

"A little nervous, to be honest," Selena's mother said.

"Understandable," said Dr. Parsons. "Please come in."

Selena still hadn't said anything to Dr. Parsons. She felt more comfortable talking to the dog.

Clover the yellow Lab turned around now and trotted along the brick pathway of the courtyard inside the high wall. Selena stood up and closed the gate securely behind her before following the others.

There had been at least two security cameras in different spots at the front of the house, and Selena saw two more inside the courtyard, aimed in separate directions.

She noticed things like that. The cameras made her feel safe, too.

Some people might see them as invasions of their privacy, but Selena wouldn't mind having a camera watching her all the time.

Something had happened to her recently—she could feel it, she *knew* it—but as hard as she tried to remember, she had no idea what it was.

And when she tried to tell the doctors that whatever

was wrong with her had started then ... once she confessed that she had no memory of it, no proof, they all acted like she was just some overdramatic teenage girl trying to pretend she had some strange disease.

Especially since none of them could find out what was wrong with her.

Even though something *definitely* was.

Selena lagged behind, not only to note the cameras, but also to take in the beauty of Dr. Parsons's courtyard. Unlike the front yard, this didn't look like the desert at all.

Trees and flowers crowded the dirt beds on both sides of the brick pathway. To the left, several lush olive trees grew tall against the wall. Beneath them bloomed masses of yellow and white daisies, red and purple pansies, and pale pink honeysuckle.

To the right of the pathway, purple sweet pea flowers climbed up a trellis set against the tan stucco house, and closer to the front door another trellis took over, where a bright magenta bougainvillea spread its arms and offered its blossoms to the sun.

Everything smelled earthy and fresh, and the flowers gave the air a light and pleasant perfume. It was spring inside the courtyard. Selena's fingers and face felt warm. Just a few minutes ago, she thought she had been enjoying the November cold, but now she liked this better. If the others weren't already inside the house, she would have stayed out here longer.

She hurried now to join them.

Clover was waiting at the open door, wagging her thick tail. Selena bent down again to pet her smooth yellow head. Then the dog led her onward into the cozy living room.

The floor was brick, covered by two large Asian rugs. Overhead the ceiling was made of dark wooden planks set between thick wooden beams.

The furnishings were homey: dark blues and forest greens for the couch and love seat and deep-cushioned chair across from them, knitted or crocheted throws draped over them in case someone got cold (Selena wasn't. The temperature in here was perfect), everything made of wood or stone or fabric, nothing cold or harsh like metal and glass.

A small, cheerful fire crackled in the brick-lined fireplace at the far end of the room. Beside it, tucked into the corner, was a plush green dog bed. It looked big enough that Selena could curl up on top of it herself, and still leave room for Clover.

"Can I get you something to drink?" Dr. Parsons offered. "Coffee, water?"

Selena and her mother both said no.

But the coffee smelled delicious, coming from the

adjoining open kitchen. Selena also smelled cinnamon. Maybe Dr. Parsons had been baking.

Natural light streamed into the kitchen from a window above the sink and from the skylight over the dark brown granite-topped island. The cabinets were all made of dark mesquite wood. The refrigerator, oven, and other appliances were all a shiny black. Two long oval braided wool rugs covered the worn oak floors on either side of the island.

Selena had never been inside a mountain cabin, but she could imagine it looking exactly like this. Right here in the middle of the city.

Everything felt comfortable and welcoming and clean.

Selena's shoulders dropped another few inches.

This was nothing like the cold and angry hospital. Nothing like any of the many doctors' offices she'd had to go to, all of their rooms so stark and loud and gritty, no matter how clean they might have looked to anyone else.

Selena had a feeling for places. She didn't talk about it much, because people thought she was weird whenever she did. But her mother at least pretended to understand.

This place ... was good. Selena could feel it in her blood.

Clover stood right up against her, leaning into Selena's leg.

"Yes," Selena told her mother. "We can stay." To Dr. Parsons: "Tell me what I have to do."

Selena pushed back the hood of her hoodie and let it fall free behind her.

"Have a seat," said Dr. Parsons. "I'll tell you what I see."

2

Dr. Winifred Parsons, age sixty-eight, Winnie to those who knew her, had resisted her calling for most of her life.

She found ways around it: pursuing her PhD in Psychology, becoming Chair of her department, writing well-respected textbooks in her field of Consumer Psychology.

She did not, as someone like her might have, assume any role in the growing field of parapsychology, also known as Consciousness Studies, Psi Research, or other equally intriguing names.

The University of Arizona, where she had spent most of her esteemed career as a professor, had a well-known and highly-regarded program for studying para-psychology and consciousness-based healthcare.

Students came from all over the world to learn what had been discovered so far—and what more could be discovered every single day—about the deep and mysterious workings of the human mind.

Despite the long and well-documented history of psi research conducted by scientists for over a century, some scientists still treated the topic as fringe. As mythology. As unworthy of receiving grant money and lab space and funds from the private sector or universities, when there were so many other, worthier and weightier discoveries that deserved time and money and attention.

But Winnie never felt that way. She admired her colleagues' research. So much so, she herself was Test Subject Number 2143, a frequent visitor to the parapsychology research lab and enthusiastic participant in all manner of experiments and studies.

As long as she could remain anonymous.

It was during one of those experiments that she met her husband Joe, gone now these past three years.

It was Joe's idea that Winnie change course. Stop pretending. Finally do what she was meant to do.

Winnie had been clairvoyant ever since she remembered. Of course, in her childhood no one called it that. They said she had visions. Prophetic dreams. Spooky knowings. Or the catch-all term, that she was psychic.

But there were a wide variety of specializations

within the psychic spectrum. Some people were gifted mediums who could communicate with those who had died. Others were medical intuitives who could identify abnormalities within a body as though they had X-Ray vision.

There were people like Winnie who could hear and see events taking place elsewhere as though watching them on a TV. Others could read minds. Some, using psychokinesis, could move physical objects through the power of their thoughts.

Winnie was not a medium. And despite trying, she had never developed the knack for psychokinesis. There were a lot of things she wasn't. But there were also several things she was, besides clairvoyant.

Like other medical intuitives, she could sometimes detect disease by envisioning herself slipping past a person's skin and into the internal structure of their body. She sometimes had flashes of visions that gave her foreknowledge of what might happen in the future.

Might, because free will was always a factor. More than once, Winnie had helped someone avert disaster simply by warning them what might come to pass.

But not everyone believed, and Winnie had to learn to accept that.

Even though at least three people had needlessly died after failing to heed her warnings. Their deaths haunted her, despite knowing in her heart that there was nothing more she could have done. Still, any loss of life was a loss to the world, and Winnie regretted it.

In addition to her other gifts, Winnie could see auras, what some people thought of as colored clouds of energy around all living things, plants and animals and people.

And this girl who had come to her this morning, Selena Martez, had one of the most damaged auras Winnie had ever seen.

People were sometimes scared to hear the truth. Winnie had to come to it slowly.

But Selena and her mother weren't here for counseling. They hadn't hired Dr. Winifred Parsons the psychologist.

They had come to Winnie the detective. The private investigator. Referred by someone Winnie knew, and who knew what she could do.

It was the only way she was willing to do business. Winnie maintained no website. She had no presence on social media. She didn't print up business cards and stick them on the notice board at a popular coffee shop.

If someone contacted her, and was willing to pay her substantial fee, then Winnie would meet with them and at least give them her initial impression based on what she felt and saw.

She didn't need the money. She and Joe had lived

comfortably on their salaries, and in retirement Winnie still had plenty of wealth to see her through.

But she knew from her decades studying consumer psychology that if she didn't charge for her services, and didn't charge a *lot*, clients wouldn't respect her. And what's more, they wouldn't believe her. When people pay a high price for services or products, they become invested in those services' or products' worth.

This car, this watch, this computer—they're the best. Highest quality.

Otherwise people would feel foolish spending so much.

If Winnie was going to invest in someone's troubles, she needed to know they would accept her advice. She had no use for anyone's skepticism. She knew what she could do.

"Let's sit down," Winnie told the mother and daughter.

She wanted to see how they arranged themselves.

The girl had already bonded with Clover. That was good. It must be why Selena chose the longer couch rather than the smaller love seat, which someone feeling too open and vulnerable would have selected.

But Selena sat boldly in the middle of the couch and Clover jumped up beside her, stretching out to fill up the space, and rested her head in Selena's lap. Selena's mother, Liz, sat on the other side.

Winnie chose the dark blue chair across from them. She slid out of her fleece-lined slippers and tucked her feet under her, then settled into the deep cushioning of the chair.

"I'll tell you what I see," she said to Selena.

She began with the good news, or at least the features that were neutral.

She described the layers of colors she could see around various parts of Selena's body: the bright red bands surrounding her waist and wrists—

"Is that bad?" Selena asked, worried.

"It isn't bad or good," Winnie assured her. "It's just you."

She described the sparks of pink puffing away from Selena's right hip, the white band around her right ankle, other hues in various places.

"But I can tell you why you feel so weak," Winnie said, finally coming to the critical information. "You're leaking. Not only a little, but a lot."

"Leaking," Liz Martez repeated. "What does that mean?"

Winnie raised her hands to her own head to demonstrate. "All around here, it's a dark charcoal gray."

"Is that bad?" Selena asked again.

This time Winnie answered, "It isn't good. But what's worse—and I'm watching it right now—" She pointed to the right side of Selena's head, the side where the dog was doing what she could by lying with her own head on Selena's lap. "—there's an open gap about eight inches long, and your energy is flowing out, like a big gash in a pipe."

Tears gathered in Selena's eyes, but through some force of will, they didn't fall.

"I knew it," she said softly. "Not *that*, but something."

"What could cause that?" Liz asked. The color had drained from her face. She clasped Selena's hand, maybe for her own security rather than the girl's.

"There's been some trauma. Psychological, rather than physical. The integrity of her mind has been breached."

Selena's dark eyes widened. Winnie could see the girl's fear. But she wouldn't try to diminish what she'd said, to talk around it as though it were normal.

It wasn't. The danger to the girl's psyche was real.

But Winnie could do something to try to repair it.

She had waited long enough for the girl and her mother to settle in and feel comfortable. Winnie couldn't bear to delay any longer. Since she first laid eyes on Selena at the front gate, she had been watching the flood of energy leaving the girl.

Winnie unfolded her legs from underneath her and stood up from the chair. "Come here. Let me help."

Selena slipped out from under Clover's sleeping head and released her mother's grip on her hand. She stood in front of Winnie on the thick blue and gold Asian rug between the couch and chair. Selena's dark brown eyes looked directly into Winnie's green.

Winnie made two claws of her hands, stiffening them into rakes.

Then beginning at Selena's feet, she began combing through the aura, as though brushing burrs and mud out of Clover's coat.

Comb, and flick. Flicking away the accumulated auric debris to keep her fingers clean.

Winnie took her time. This process should never be rushed. She raked inch by inch up the front of Selena's legs, holding her fingers about six inches out from the girl's body where the colors of the aura were most visible, then she shifted around Selena to the back and repeated the process there.

Over the years Winnie had met other clairvoyants with their own methods for clearing and repairing auras, but this way had always worked for her. She hoped it was enough to help Selena.

When the legs were cleared, Winnie moved on to Selena's waist, chest, back, and arms.

Throughout, the girl stood calm and silent, sometimes watching Winnie work, sometimes closing her eyes briefly before snapping them open again, as though she'd accidentally fallen asleep.

The girl's entire torso now smoothed of its ragged

lines, all the way up to her shoulders, Winnie paused for a moment and stepped back. She wanted to see what progress they had made.

Dark charcoal-gray energy continued to pour from the gaping hole near Selena's head. The energy field there looked tattered and delicate all along its edges.

Winnie would have to be careful. She didn't want to rip the hole any wider. Instead she wanted to coax the wound closed.

She locked eyes with Selena. She could see on the girl's face that Selena's curiosity had given way to fear again.

"This won't hurt," Winnie assured her.

"I know," said Selena. "I can already feel it. How much better it is already."

"You can?" Liz asked, amazed. Selena nodded. From Liz's vantage, the whole display must have seemed like nothing but theater.

Whether she believed Winnie had really done anything or not, Liz seemed relieved that at least her child felt better.

"But this..." Selena said to Winnie, lifting her hand to the right side of her head. Gray energy poured around it and between Selena's fingers, like water coursing around the rocks in a river. "Do you really think you can fix it?"

"Not permanently," Winnie said. All of her clients

paid her for the truth. "We'll have to find the cause first. But maybe I can slow it down for now."

Selena drew a deep breath and closed her eyes. Winnie got back to work.

She felt like a seamstress, picking up loose tendrils of Selena's gaping energy field and gently joining them back together. She worked slowly, methodically, pinching the tattered edges inch by inch, until she felt confident that the seams would hold. For now.

Then she returned to combing, smoothing, moving the stale, diseased charcoal energy away, hoping to encourage new life in the field, freshening it with contributions from her own.

Selena's cranial aura was pale pink now, not as vibrant as Winnie wanted it to be, but it was an improvement. It was progress.

Selena's breath had become shallow for a while, but now she seemed to be breathing normally again.

The girl opened her eyes. "Is it done?"

"You tell me."

Winnie returned to her seat. Selena remained standing, breathing deeply, assessing.

"How do you feel, honey?" Liz asked.

"Better," Selena said. "Much better. Except, here..." She pointed to her right temple. She was right: Winnie could see the spot, too.

A black dot, about the size of a quarter, hovered

close to Selena's temple, hard to see against her dark brown hair.

Winnie stood again and came closer. She reached out for the black dot, but it faded before she could touch it.

When she moved backward, the dot reappeared. She tried once again to capture it, but the spot faded out of view.

Winnie shook her head. "I can't get it. But that isn't necessarily bad. It might fade away on its own."

"Does it hurt?" Liz asked her.

Selena rubbed her right temple. "A little. Yes. Like there's a bruise here."

She leaned over so her mother could examine it for herself. Liz gently smoothed back Selena's hair and stared at the unblemished skin.

But Winnie could see the spot again, the same size and color.

She had never seen that after a smoothing. She didn't know what it meant.

"That's the first step," she told Selena. "Now, it's time to find out what this is all about."

"I want to be—I'm *going to be*—an astronaut," Selena answered Dr. Parsons's first question.

Dr. Parsons smiled. "I'm glad to hear it."

Selena studied the doctor's face. She was used to adults chuckling when she told them of her ambition. Astronaut. It sounded so impossible.

But Selena had wanted it, dreamed of it, *pursued* it, since she was six years old. She wasn't joking. This wasn't some frivolous idea, the way some of her classmates switched from wanting to be a lawyer ... no, a veterinarian ... an NFL player ... a teacher ... "I just want to be *rich*!"

It was all so boring.

There were steps to take. Real life, actual steps. And Selena had researched them since she was a little girl.

Ever since she saw a program on PBS about women astronauts. She knew then, like you're born with certain fingerprints and DNA. She was born to be an astronaut. Search over.

She took all the hardest math and science classes school offered. Right now she was in AP Physics, Advanced Calculus, and a robotics class offered as an elective.

Robots would be used for space travel. They already were. The University of Arizona Lunar and Planetary Sciences department was responsible for the Mars Rover, the robot currently exploring all over Mars.

It was why Selena was applying there. To be part of a program like *that*. When NASA was looking for new astronauts, they would look at Selena's list of accomplishments and think wow, we want *her*.

Selena would be ready for the future—for her future. She was leaving nothing to chance.

"You know," Dr. Parsons said, setting down her pen. She had been taking notes all along on a pastel blue legal pad. Selena liked the color. She didn't know they came in anything but canary yellow. "When the realtor sold us this house, she said Frank Borman used to live here as a child. I don't know if it's true—"

"Frank Borman, the astronaut?" Selena said.

"That's the one," Dr. Parsons answered.

Selena looked around the living room again. It was fate. The idea of it gave her chills.

Dr. Parsons picked up her pen again. "Tell me about your classes."

Selena described all six of them, then went on to talk about the teachers. The robotics class was taught by Ellie Nuy, a grad student from the U of A who knew all about the Mars program.

Mr. Spence was the AP Physics teacher. This was the first time Selena had been in one of his classes. He only taught seniors, and always took the best of the best.

So Selena had been thrilled when, after just two weeks into the semester, Mr. Spence invited her to join his Genius Track. Everyone knew that was practically impossible to get into.

There were only seven kids in it total, out of the AP Physics class of twenty. Selena and Brandy Ochoa were the only two girls. Selena had gone to school with Brandy since first grade. She knew the girl was brilliant.

But Brandy wanted to be an inventor. She was in the robotics class, too.

As far as Selena knew, she was the only one in the Genius Track who was planning on being an astronaut and traveling the stars.

Dr. Parsons checked her watch. "I'm hungry. How about you?"

Time had flown by. It was almost noon.

"I made cinnamon rolls before you came," said Dr. Parsons. "Let's take a break."

Clover had been snoring the whole time with her head in Selena's lap. Selena hated to wake the dog, but the truth was, she was starving.

That had been one of her symptoms this past month: no appetite at all. Along with extreme lethargy and a scary inability to focus to mind. She was constantly wandering off topic in her thoughts, forgetting what she was supposed to be studying. She had to reread and reread her assignments, trying to force the information into her head.

She got a C-minus on her calculus test—something that had never happened before—and Selena realized in a panic that same day that she couldn't understand what Mr. Spence was saying about all of the physics calculations he'd written up on the board.

That was when she finally told her mother what was going on.

Selena's dreams for the future were slipping away faster than she could stop them.

But now. Now she was feeling hopeful again.

Maybe Dr. Parsons really could cure her. Whatever this was.

Dr. Parsons made a fresh pot of coffee, and she and Selena's mother drank some to go with their rolls. Selena just wanted water to wash down the delicious sugar. Then the break was over, and it was back to the couch.

Selena settled in, and Clover found her spot again.

Dr. Parsons picked up her pad and paper. She had more questions. Lots of questions.

It wasn't like with the other doctors. They asked questions, too, but most of them only pretended to hear what Selena said. She could tell they already knew what tests they were going to order. They already thought they knew what must be wrong.

But Dr. Parsons actually listened. Selena could tell that she heard.

She trusted Selena to know what it felt like to be inside her own body, what it felt like to think with her own mind.

Finally Dr. Parsons finished with all her questions.

She tilted her head and looked at Selena with those calm green eyes.

"How do you feel about being hypnotized?" asked Dr. Parsons.

Selena's mother had already warned her that would probably be part of this session.

Selena nodded. She didn't trust her voice. The truth was, the idea of being put in a trance, or whatever it was, scared her. Scared her a lot.

It was why she never smoked weed or drank beer, even though some of her friends did. Selena valued her mind. She liked feeling in control. She didn't want to mess it up and maybe lose the brain cells she needed to achieve her childhood goal.

Dr. Parsons leaned forward and reached out her hand.

Selena reached her hand out to meet it.

Dr. Parsons looked into Selena's eyes and squeezed her fingers. "I promise. I won't do anything you don't want."

"But ... you think it will help," Selena said. "Maybe ... help me remember."

"I do," said Dr. Parsons.

"And I'll be right here, baby," Selena's mother said.

Selena blew out a tense breath. "Okay. Let's do it."

4

The girl was a good candidate for hypnotism. Intelligent, curious, imaginative.

Clover moved to her dog bed and Liz shifted over to the love seat so Selena could stretch out the full length of the couch.

Winnie had used hypnotism for years to help her family and friends with assorted problems. People quit smoking, cured their insomnia, discovered the source of their anxiety—her nephew Danny even got over his fear of flying.

And her late husband Joe had depended on Winnie's skill with hypnotism to help him manage certain aspects of his work.

For the past three years, as Winnie gained more and more clients through her referral-only business, she had

had more opportunities than ever before to practice using this valuable tool.

So it was with confidence that she began leading the girl down into the first layer of trance. Selena sank there easily, gently. Everything was as expected.

Liz sat on the edge of the love seat, elbows on her knees, hands clasped in front of her mouth. She seemed to be barely breathing as she watched her daughter sink ever deeper into these rarely visited chambers of the mind.

"Are you still with me?" Dr. Parsons softly asked.

"Yes," Selena answered. In contrast to her mother, Selena breathed normally. Her color was good. She looked relaxed and well.

When Winnie was certain the girl was deep enough, she began bringing her deeper still.

Down to the next layer of consciousness where people often harbored their secret fears.

Here were the mysteries behind certain illnesses. Here were the sources of phobias and the troubling beliefs that might torment someone all of their life.

"Why are you sick?" Winnie asked Selena.

The girl didn't answer.

Winnie rephrased her question. "What is the cause of the problems with this body?"

Selena mumbled something Winnie didn't hear.

Liz leaned even further forward. "What did she say?"

"Please repeat that," Winnie said quietly.

Selena did. "Shall not."

Winnie and Liz exchanged a look.

"What is the cause of the problems with this body?" Winnie asked.

"Shall not," Selena answered again.

Winnie tried other questions. Always to receive the same answer.

Shall not.

There was a barrier in the girl's mind.

How it got there … whether it was *placed* there … and if so, by whom…

Could the girl have erected that barrier herself? If so, why? What was so terrible that she didn't want herself to know?

In all of her years, Winnie had never heard of anything like this.

After ten more minutes of trying, she realized there was no point in badgering the girl. Selena's answer was always the same.

Winnie brought her carefully out of the trance.

Selena rubbed her eyes, then turned her head to look at her mother and Winnie.

"Did you get anything?" she asked.

"Yes," Winnie said. It was the truth.

She just didn't know what the truth meant.

5

Selena could tell something had gone wrong. Her mother wouldn't meet her eye.

"Mom? What happened?" Selena sat up, alarmed by the unreadable look on her mother's face.

Dr. Parsons told her about the hypnotism. About what Selena said. *Shall not.* What was that supposed to mean?

"You've never heard anyone say that?" asked Dr. Parsons.

"No," Selena said. "It sounds weird. I would remember."

Then she thought a moment.

"Wouldn't I?"

She pressed her palms against her temples, as though she could somehow force her brain to work.

Then she remembered the black dot Dr. Parsons had seen near her right temple. Selena dropped her hands and asked Dr. Parsons if it was still there.

Dr. Parsons stared at the right side of Selena's head and nodded.

"So what *is* it?" Selena asked, her voice sounding shrill to her own ears. She didn't feel safe anymore. Her heart had picked up speed and was now banging against her ribs.

Selena's mother came over to sit beside her and wrap her arm around Selena's shoulders.

"Doctor—" her mother started to say, but Dr. Parsons was deep in thought.

Selena squeezed her mother's knee. She didn't want to interrupt the doctor if she might be close to some kind of solution.

At last Dr. Parsons looked up. "What time is school tomorrow?"

Today was the Sunday after Thanksgiving. The four-day break was almost over.

Selena had slept most of the time, until this morning. Now she was wide awake.

"Seven-fifty," she answered.

"Do your friends know your grandmother?" Dr. Parsons asked. She had already made a list of all of Selena's family.

"No, she lives in Seattle," Selena said.

"Good," said Dr. Parsons. "I'll be her. I'll meet you in front of the school tomorrow."

6

Older people were already irrelevant and invisible. Winnie didn't need much of a disguise.

Brown contacts, wire-rim glasses, a salt and pepper wig to cover her blonde-white hair.

She wouldn't need makeup. That would only draw attention to her face.

She kept a wardrobe of old lady clothes for occasions just like this. Brown and pink paisley blouse, brown knit slacks, thin socks, brown flats with rubber soles to help with her unsteady elderly walk.

No cane, that was too memorable. A small brown purse with a handle in the center, just like her own grandmother used to carry.

"Whoa," Selena said when she walked up to meet her.

"Am I Gran, Grandma, or Nana?"

"Nan," Selena said.

"Walk slowly. Let me take your arm."

The two of them set off at a maddeningly slow pace toward Selena's first class.

Winnie had already walked Clover this morning from their house to a loop around the U of A campus. But that was Dr. Winifred Parsons. She was Selena's Nan now.

"Can you see everyone's auras?" Selena asked as they made their way through the crowded hallways.

"If I wanted to," Winnie said, "yes. But it's like trying to watch all the channels on your TV at the same time. It's better to focus on one at a time, and only if I want the information."

The crowded high school was hectic, but Winnie loved the energy of being around students again. The children passing to and fro all around her looked so much younger than any of the college students she used to teach.

But they were all the same, in their way: self-conscious, desperate for approval, some of them needy, some cocky, but all of them seeking validation that they mattered—to their peers, to their teachers, to their families and friends, to the world.

Winnie had loved being a professor. She loved seeing the spark in her students' eyes.

She had retired not because she grew tired of it, the way many of her colleagues came to feel.

On a morning four years ago, she rolled over in bed to snuggle up to her husband. Her clairvoyant vision flashed, and she saw a mass inside Joe's liver. It was the first moment either of them knew that he was sick.

When the diagnosis came, Winnie immediately knew what she would do.

She loved her career, she loved teaching, she loved exploring the mysteries of the mind.

But she loved Joe infinitely more. She retired and spent his last year helping him through to the end.

The night before he died, he came to her in a vision.

Whether he knew he was doing it, or whether he was already too far gone to reach out to her on his own, Winnie treasured that last conversation. For the two weeks before it, Joe had been in and out of a coma and unable to speak.

She had told no one what he said. It was too precious to give away to anyone else. Winnie locked it away in her heart and did exactly what Joe encouraged her to do.

And she had been doing it for the past three years. The widow Dr. Parsons.

Although she might look fondly at these children

around her, and feel nostalgic for her days as a professor, Winnie didn't regret her decision. Joe was right. This was her path.

But how things had changed since she had been in high school herself. The metal detectors at the entrances, no more lockers ("It's because of drugs," Selena explained. "And weapons."), kids pulling wheeled backpacks as big as carry-on luggage, children hugging much more than Winnie ever remembered seeing in her own youth or at the university.

Selena hugged people, too. Sometimes she kissed her friends on the cheek and received a kiss back.

There was far more open affection than Winnie was accustomed to—whether it was heart-felt or not.

"Yeah, I don't really like her," Selena explained about one girl. "But if I don't hug her every time I see her, she gets all moody and crazy dramatic."

As always, Winnie appreciated no longer being young.

Selena had three classes in the morning, then a half-hour lunch break, then three more classes in the afternoon.

At the beginning of each class, Selena introduced her Nan to the teacher and asked if it was all right for her to sit at the back of the class and watch.

"I miss my girl," Winnie said each time, giving

Selena a one-armed squeeze and adding her own kiss to the girl's already-kissed cheek.

"Of course," each teacher said, although Winnie could see that not all of them felt comfortable being observed.

But Mr. Spence, the AP Physics teacher, positively reveled in it.

Winnie could see his aura brighten the moment he realized he'd have another member in his audience.

"Nan," he said, taking Winnie's hand in his own. He was in his early fifties, tall, too thin, and with a thick thatch of black hair that couldn't be natural, had to be dyed.

Winnie didn't care for the man's touch. It was dry and not clammy, but it felt amphibious just the same.

Winnie extracted her hand as soon as she could and ambled toward the back of the room.

AP Physics was Selena's fifth-period class. Winnie could feel her own energy beginning to lag. It had been a long time since she had to sit through high school math and English and science classes, and she couldn't say she enjoyed them, even though the teachers were generally good.

She was looking forward the last class of the day, robotics. That was something new. Until then, she could endure a physics lecture for the sake of her young client.

Winnie lowered herself into one of the hard plastic

seats behind the other students. Then Mr. Spence began his show.

Physics had never been one of Winnie's passions. She preferred biology, especially botany.

She could feel her mind wandering as Mr. Spence spoke of concepts and terms that had no meaning in Winnie's life. His voice boomed sometimes, enthusiastically, and the few times he caught Winnie off guard and made her look up, he always locked eyes with her and smiled, as though expecting her approval.

Selena was sitting at the far left of the room, close to the windows.

In the shifting afternoon sunlight, Winnie didn't see at first what she saw now.

The gash in the girl's cranial aura had broken open again, and dark gray energy was spewing out.

Winnie rose to her feet in alarm. She forgot to be Nan, and was Dr. Parsons.

She hurried to Selena's side and quickly whispered, "We have to go."

She tugged at the girl's arm when it appeared Selena felt too embarrassed to just get up and leave.

"Is everything all right?" Mr. Spence asked, frowning. Winnie had ruined the flow of his performance.

"I'm not feeling well," Winnie said, remembering to sound frail. "I forgot my pills. Selena needs to take me home."

Selena was on her feet now, but Winnie could see the girl wasn't right.

Her eyes seemed unfocused. The hand Winnie held onto felt limp.

Charcoal energy continued spilling from the right side of Selena's head. The black dot that had been the size of a quarter yesterday now looked the size of an egg.

Winnie helped the girl up the aisle, then across the front of the room, in front of Mr. Spence.

He had lost all of his earlier congeniality, and now scowled at Selena and Winnie as they made their way toward the door.

"You're falling behind," he warned Selena.

She turned back, a look of anguish on her face.

"Shame on you," Nan Winnie told him. She knew a bully when she saw one.

By the time they reached the hallway, tears spilled down Selena's cheeks.

But Winnie had no time to comfort her here. The hole in her cranial aura was getting worse.

Winnie gave up walking like an old woman. She braced her arm around Selena and guided the girl out of the school.

"Sit here," Winnie said, leaving Selena on a concrete bench near the parking lot. "I'll be back in a minute. Just wait."

Winnie race-walked toward her car. She could feel

her heart speeding, but her mind was working just as fast.

It was that teacher, Mr. Spence. He was the danger, although Winnie didn't know how.

It would be easy to work up a hatred for the man, just from seeing his effect on Selena.

But Winnie calmed her heart and bridled her mind. Anger would not help her now.

She had seen for herself what was making her client sick.

Now it was Winnie's job to help her.

7

Selena lay on Dr. Parsons's couch with a cool washcloth over her forehead.

She drew up her knees to make room for Clover, who leapt up and tucked herself on top of Selena's feet.

"Your mother will be here soon," said Dr. Parsons. She squeezed Selena's hand.

Selena's head hurt so much, she didn't want to open her eyes. She could feel a hot tear slide down her cheek.

She was worse, not better. Worse than before.

She felt like throwing up, the pain was so bad.

Before long she heard the doorbell. It was like a gong inside her head.

Then her mother was beside her, speaking softly, and obviously scared.

"Let's begin," said Dr. Parsons. "Selena, can you hear me?"

Then the pain disappeared and everything went black.

8

Winnie's fingers shook. She pressed them against her lap and sat up straight.

She had had a taste of the man, Mr. Spence. If he was the cause of Selena's illness, Winnie would learn it.

She could well imagine the girl being afraid of him, and causing herself psychological trauma as a result.

Selena led a stressful life. She had set a high bar for herself. Maybe too high. A full and difficult class load. The pressure of getting into college. The pressure of living up to her grand expectations.

The body was wise. It had ways of demanding attention to force its owner to correct a dangerous course.

The mind could sometimes fool itself, but the body would not allow the deception to go on for too long.

It acted in its own self-interest. The body wanted to

live. To do that, it needed to keep its mind and its spirit healthy and whole.

Someone like Winnie could see the body's distress as the intact aura around it broke apart. She could see the black mark of an invading threat, like the one that hovered near Selena's right temple.

Winnie was not as skilled as some of the medical intuitives she had met over the years, but she could see inside a body if she tried hard enough.

Or sometimes, as with Joe, the vision might come to her whether she wanted it or not.

Back at the school, as Winnie had helped Selena into the passenger seat of her car, she saw inside the girl's body in a flash of clarity.

Selena was healthy and whole. There was nothing physically wrong with her.

What was wrong was whatever had attacked her mind.

The gash in her cranial aura was real. It wasn't something Winnie or another clairvoyant would imagine.

The auric body was as real as the flesh beneath it. It was as real as radio waves and infrared light, even though ordinary human eyes couldn't detect them.

Something had happened to Selena. Winnie didn't believe it was simply the girl's stress. A smart, ambitious girl like Selena wouldn't simply fall apart without a reason.

Winnie had asked all the questions she could. Neither Selena nor her mother could offer a compelling answer.

The answer lay within Selena's mind, hidden behind the words *Shall not.*

If Winnie could not pass that barrier, like before, then she would have to be sneaky this time.

9

You're falling behind.

Selena gasped and sat up.

The damp washcloth fell from her head. She dropped it onto the brick floor.

Clover the yellow Lab lifted her head and raised her ears.

Selena reached over and stroked the pretty girl's face.

Her headache was gone. She raised her right hand to her head. She poked her index finger into the hole.

It was gooey in there. Like syrup. Or tar. Selena pulled out her finger and the sticky black goo came with it.

She sniffed it. It smelled burnt. Disgusting. She retrieved the washcloth and wiped her finger clean.

Her mother had been here, she thought. And Dr. Parsons, sitting in her chair.

You're falling behind.

Shall NOT.

Where have you heard that before?

Selena turned at a sound behind her.

You're falling behind.

I'm sorry. I'll make it up.

I haven't been feeling well...

Shall *not.*

Where have you heard that before?

Here, Selena said. Here.

She lay on her back on an inflatable pad, in a room that felt familiar.

Brandy Ochoa lay on a pad beside her. She was sleeping. But then she wasn't. Now Brandy was talking.

Talking to a woman. A woman Selena didn't know. The woman looked up and saw Selena watching.

"Roy?" the woman turned and called over her shoulder.

Shall not.

The woman said that to Brandy Ochoa.

The man whose name must be Roy stood behind Selena's inflated pad and looked down at her. His face was upside down.

Roy was Mr. Spence.

"Give her more," he said. "I'm not ready."

"Well hurry up," the woman said. "Look at the time."

You're falling behind.

I know. I'm sorry. I'll catch up. Don't kick me out.

"Hold on," the woman said, "I'm almost finished. I'll just get to her now."

Shall not, the woman told Brandy. Then she crawled over to Selena's pad.

"What did you and Dr. Lindeman discuss?" the woman asked.

Dr. Lindeman was a professor in the University of Arizona's Lunar and Planetary Sciences department. Selena had met with him over the summer to discuss what studies she might pursue there.

Her mother knew someone who knew Dr. Lindeman, and he had been generous with his time.

He had a daughter who was an aerospace engineer. For a while she worked at NASA. Dr. Lindeman told Selena about some of her work. He said he would set up a meeting between the two of them when his daughter came home to visit for Christmas.

A reflection caught Selena's eye. She turned to the right to see what it was. A video camera sat near her head, the beady eye of its lens aimed at her face.

"What did you and Dr. Lindeman discuss?" the woman asked again.

"I ... don't remember," Selena said.

The woman sighed. "Try harder."

Selena glanced to her left, to where Brandy Ochoa lay asleep.

Then she looked beyond, to the rest of the room.

She had been here before, at the beginning of the semester. No, two weeks after, when Mr. Spence threw a party.

It was for the seven kids in his Genius Track, and for their parents. Selena and her mother had gone.

This was his living room. Selena recognized the big leather couch and the TV that took up most of the wall in front of it.

Ramon Wing was lying on the couch now. There were more inflated pads in spots around the room.

Selena could see the five boys. Mr. Spence was kneeling beside Kieran and talking to him. There was a camera pointed at Kieran's head.

The woman snapped her fingers over Selena's face. "Hey. Answer me. We're almost out of time."

She had red hair. She looked about Selena's mom's age. Her face was greasy. She was sweating.

"I'm tired," Selena said. She closed her eyes. She hoped the woman would go away.

The woman sighed again. "You get anything?" she called out.

"Plenty," Mr. Spence answered. "Let's finish."

"Okay, my pretty," the woman said to Selena. "You know the drill. Thou shalt not—"

"You shall not," Mr. Spence corrected her.

"You shall not remember," the woman said. "You shall not tell anyone what you heard or saw here. You shall not tell anyone about me or Roy. If you try, it will hurt you. If you ever say anything about this, you're dead."

"Don't embellish," said Mr. Spence. "Stick to the script. Repet—"

"Repetition," the woman said. "I know."

Then she and Mr. Spence spoke together, saying, "Micky Mouse surfs in Fiji."

Selena's vision went black.

Winnie opened her eyes.

It was the prerogative of the clairvoyant to ride along.

Winnie used whatever tools she had. If Selena could not answer Winnie's questions about what was in her mind, then Winnie had to trick Selena into reliving the event in secret.

Winnie attached her mind to Selena's, so that she could watch it through Selena's eyes.

Winnie had seen enough bad hypnosis to know what that phrase about Mickey Mouse was for.

The hypnotist wanted to implant a phrase for next time, to make it easier to put the subject into a trance.

But you don't want to pick a phrase anyone might say in casual conversation. You don't want your subject going under without you there.

Mickey Mouse surfs in Fiji. Unlikely that anyone would accidentally say it.

But a bad hypnotist would need more than a clever phrase. He would probably use drugs to keep his subject compliant.

Winnie heard it through Selena's ears. Roy Spence telling his accomplice, "Give her more. I'm not ready."

That sounded like drugs to Winnie. But there was more to what she saw.

The Genius Track. Who were those kids? What were their ambitions? Where were they going to end up?

Selena was stirring. She still seemed groggy. Winnie would have to let her rest for now.

But Selena and her mother were counting on Winnie to uncover the truth. Winnie thought she was closer now.

Selena opened her eyes. Clover thumped her tail against the couch.

Selena yawned. She seemed fairly alert. And the rip in her aura had closed enough on its own that the energy loss was now only a trickle.

Maybe it was safe to ask Selena more questions. Winnie would watch her closely to make sure.

"What is the Genius Track? How long has that been going on?"

"For years," Selena said. "It's a huge honor. Mr.

Spence still has old students who come back and visit him. They're big deals. Why?"

Winnie handed her a notepad and pen. "Can you make me a list?"

Selena could only come up with twenty for now. Winnie didn't recognize any of the names.

"Who are they?" she asked.

"Scientists, mostly. Some of them work at NASA. That Alstead guy designs cars. If you want, I can look up the rest of them. There's a list in Mr. Spence's room."

"I don't want you going back there," Winnie said.

Then she described everything she saw to Selena and her mother.

Liz gaped at her, mouth open. Then she pressed her lips together and covered them with her hand.

Selena stared at Winnie, grim-faced. She shook her head. "That evil bastard."

"Why?" Liz asked. "Why would he do that?"

"Maybe he can sell the information," Winnie said.

"But we're just kids," said Selena.

"Now," Winnie agreed. "But when you're an astronaut, think of all the knowledge you'll have by then. If some other government wanted it, or some private entrepreneur..."

"So I go back and visit good old Mr. Spence, and he gives me a drug and hypnotizes me and I tell him everything I know."

Selena stood up from the couch. She held her arms tight at her sides.

Winnie could see the glow around the girl. Red hot, with bands of yellow.

The black disk that had been left as a badge near her temple was gone now, completely faded away.

Roy Spence's power over at least one victim was gone. Now Winnie would make sure the other victims were freed.

She had friends with resources unlike her own. Not clairvoyants, but officers of the law.

She would assemble her facts. Gather the evidence. And then let others make sure that justice was done.

"Should I tell Brandy not to go this Saturday?" Selena asked.

"What's Saturday?" Winnie asked.

"It's when the Genius Track meets at Mr. Spence's house."

Saturday. If Winnie worked quickly now, she could make sure it was a meeting Roy Spence would never forget.

"So ... is it over?" Liz asked. "Is she going to be all right?"

She held out her hand for Selena, who took it. The girl sat on the love seat beside her mother. The red hot ring around her had muted down to a pale rose.

The rip near Selena's head had completely closed.

"Ask Selena," Winnie said. "How do you feel?"

The girl closed her eyes and drew a deep breath.

"I think …" Selena paused and looked around the room. "Did an astronaut really live here?"

"Let's assume he did," Winnie said. "That realtor had no reason to make it up."

"So then you bought this house. And one day I came here … a future astronaut. And you helped me." Selena smiled. "It's kind of perfect."

Winnie smiled, too. "It's almost as if I'm psychic."

A MAN OF APPETITES

1

"Aunt Winnie, do you already know what your present is?" Annabelle asked.

Dr. Winifred Parsons's six-year-old grandniece held out a wrapped Christmas gift to Winnie.

"I don't," Winnie said. "Do you?"

"Uh-huh, I helped pick it out. But Mom said you'll probably guess before you open it. You know everything."

Winnie laughed. "*Everything*? That's quite a claim."

"Well," said Annabelle, "*most* things."

There were only four of them gathered for Christmas breakfast this year: Winnie, her niece Rose, Rose's husband Matthew, and their daughter Annabelle.

Or really, there were five of them.

Clover, Winnie's yellow Labrador, lay on her plush

green dog bed near the fireplace, patiently wearing a pair of reindeer antlers that Winnie put on her before the guests arrived.

Annabelle sat on the dog bed, too, with her arm around Clover. Yellow dog hair clung to Annabelle's forest-green tights, but nobody cared. This home was a place for people and dogs to relax. No one minded the hairy legs.

Winnie sat cross-legged on the floor beside the girl and dog, sipping coffee from a Santa mug and warming her back against the brick hearth. The morning was cold by Tucson standards, just forty-two degrees, so Winnie made a blazing fire before her family arrived.

Usually the group included her nephew Danny and his wife and kids, too, but they were all away in even colder Seattle visiting his in-laws.

Winnie had already bundled up at dawn and walked Clover around the nearby University of Arizona campus, then came home and finished making cinnamon rolls and sour cream coffee cake.

There were other foods, too, quiche and and hash browns and fruit, but they were just side dishes. Sugar was always the main course.

Winnie set aside her coffee and reached for Annabelle. "Bring the present, too."

Annabelle climbed onto Winnie's lap and snuggled back against her grandaunt.

Christmas had always been Winnie's husband Joe's favorite holiday. The Santa mug had been his, as was the Santa hat that Winnie wore this morning over her chin-length white-blonde hair. She also wore one of Joe's old flannel shirts, a green plaid for the festive color.

Joe had been gone for three Christmases now. Winnie still missed him every day. But having her family here gave the holiday a precious and cheerful glow.

"Tell me the story," Annabelle said. "Then you can have your present." She tucked the crinkly package under her elbows as though Winnie might dare to take it.

Winnie rested her chin on top of the girl's soft brown hair. She could smell Annabelle's strawberry-scented shampoo.

"You've heard it a hundred times," Matthew said. At forty-one, he still had a boyish look about him, with an easily-provoked smile and perpetually tousled brown hair.

"But it's my favorite," Annabelle told her father.

"That's funny," Winnie said, "it's my favorite, too."

She smiled fondly at Rose. Her niece, a lawyer, was a year younger than Matthew. With her strawberry-blonde hair and green eyes, she looked so much like her father, Winnie's brother Steven, Winnie could sometimes see Steven's face overlaying Rose's.

Rose and Matthew sat on the thick Asian rug near

the hearth, amidst the wrappings and presents. Rose leaned back against Matthew's knees. He wrapped his arms around her as they all settled in for annual retelling of the family story.

"Seven Christmases ago," Winnie began, "your mother and father came here for breakfast, just like today."

"And Grandpa was sitting right there," Annabelle said, pointing to the dark blue deep-cushioned chair in the middle of the living room.

"He was right there," Winnie agreed, picturing him now. The tall, silver-haired, Air Force Colonel wearing his pressed khaki pants, a red flannel shirt, and the snowman slippers Rose had bought him some previous Christmas.

He also wore his Santa hat and drank coffee from the same mug Winnie had brought out this morning, just for the occasion.

Clover was only a pup then. Joe had tried to set the reindeer antlers on her head, but she shook them off and dug her teeth into them before Joe could swiftly snatch them away.

The ones Clover wore now were that same pair. Winnie had sewn closed the hole at the base of one of the antlers where Clover's puppy teeth had bored into the stuffing.

"And you answered the door," Annabelle prompted. "And you saw my mom and you said—"

Annabelle and Winnie said it together. "Oh! You're pregnant!"

It had come to Winnie in a flash, as information often did: an image of the baby girl that Rose would be holding the following Christmas.

"And my mom didn't know," Annabelle said.

"I didn't," Rose agreed.

"And Daddy didn't either."

"Not at all," Matthew said.

"But Grandpa said..."

Winnie could still see him, jumping up from his chair, laughing merrily as he strode toward them to hug Rose and Matthew.

"Your grandpa said, 'Do you know how hard it is to keep a secret from her?' He'd been holding it in all morning, purposely trying to block it from his mind. He already knew before all of us, because the night before he heard me talking about you in my sleep. *Annabelle*, he heard me say..."

"Yes," Annabelle said. She sighed with contentment and collapsed back into Winnie. Rose and Winnie exchanged a smile.

"Now she gets her present," Matthew reminded his daughter.

"Oh!" Annabelle twisted around and handed the package to Winnie.

It was true, Winnie already did know what was inside. But that didn't make it any less fun to unwrap.

"Socks! Let's see what kind."

Her family had indulged her this year with four pairs, all of them thick and fuzzy and colorful.

"You know just what I like," she told the little girl, and gave her an extra squeeze.

She saw Rose elbow Matthew.

Matthew cleared his throat.

Winnie set the socks on her lap. "Oh, now, what is it?"

She knew some things, but not everything. Despite her array of extraordinary gifts—clairvoyance, occasional medical intuition, foresight and visions like the one about Rose's pregnancy—Winnie could still be surprised, and often was.

Pleasantly so or not.

"Matthew has a favor to ask you," Rose said. "A big one."

From the look of discomfort on Matthew's face, Winnie guessed she wouldn't like it too much.

"I don't know if you've followed the news at all," Matthew said, "but our district just awarded a major construction contract to Bradley Klader. Have you heard of him?"

"Vaguely," Winnie said. "Go on." She had a flash of a fifty-ish, stocky blond man in a tuxedo, looking like a hockey player dressed for his wedding.

"On paper," Matthew said, "everything seems fine. But ... I don't know. I just have the feeling something's off. And you told me I should always pay attention to feelings like that."

"And so you should," Winnie agreed.

Matthew was the superintendent of Tucson's largest school district. It was how he met Rose. At the time, he was the school district's in-house lawyer, but when a group of parents sued one of the high schools, he knew he needed outside counsel.

Rose not only won the case, she fell in love as well.

"I've met him, too," Rose said. "Just a quick hello when I met Matthew for lunch, and Klader was leaving their meeting. Matthew introduced me, and..." Rose shivered. "Just made my skin crawl."

"Like bugs?" Annabelle asked.

"Like worms," Rose told her. "All over me."

"Yuck," said Annabelle.

Winnie was still thinking of the man in the tuxedo. Even though she had never seen him before, she assumed that was Klader. Sometimes just hearing a name would bring that person's face into her mind.

"So here's the favor," Matthew said. "Klader throws a New Year's Eve ball every year—"

"A ball?" Annabelle asked. "Like Cinderella?"

"I wish," her mother said. "It's probably more like a bunch of fancy people standing around drinking and bragging about all their money. Which is why I prefer to stay home with you."

Rose stole a mischievous glance at Winnie. Winnie could guess what was coming next.

"I'm asking you, dear Aunt," Matthew said formally, "to be my date. I'd like to know what you think of him."

Winnie raised her left eyebrow. "How fancy?"

"That's the bad part," Matthew confessed. "It's a black and white ball. Black tie and gowns."

"You're right," Winnie said. "This is a *very* big favor."

When she retired from being a professor four years ago, she gave away all of her professional-looking clothes.

And after Joe's funeral, she got rid of any stitch of clothing that was black. She wouldn't wear black again, even for Matthew.

"Matthew will have to rent a tux," Rose said. "We don't usually have the need. I don't assume you have anything..."

"Absolutely not."

"I can go shopping with you if you want," Rose offered.

Winnie smiled. "Absolutely not."

She knew just where to go. She could be in and out

of there in under half an hour. She prided herself on that skill.

"I can pay you, of course," Matthew said. "I want to officially hire you."

Winnie appreciated the offer. She had no doubt that Matthew was sincere. Winnie made a nice living now by using her gifts to help others uncover hidden truths.

But she didn't need the money. As a Doctor of Psychology for the past three and a half decades, with a specialty in Consumer Psychology, Winnie had studied the effect of pricing on the consumer mind.

Many people felt strange, even foolish, approaching a psychic for help. They wouldn't admit it to their friends and family. They often came to Winnie in secret.

But charging them the same fee that a lawyer or medical doctor might charge took some of the sting away. Paying handsomely for her services helped them see Winnie as a legitimate specialist who could help them with their problems.

Often, with many of her clients, Winnie still felt tempted to do her work for free. She knew that some of them would struggle to pay her substantial bill.

But she would rather let them pay her in small amounts over time than delete the bill entirely. If she behaved as though her advice had no value, some of her clients would doubt that value as well. And then whatever answers she brought them would begin to seem suspect.

Her clients would no longer believe that what Winnie told them was the truth. And Winnie prided herself on working on a problem until she did in fact uncover that truth.

Her family, including Rose's husband Matthew, already knew what Winnie could do. None of them doubted her for a moment.

She wouldn't dream of charging them a penny.

"Don't be silly, dear," she told Matthew. "Merry Christmas. You have yourself a date."

2

Winnie had no illusions that she could compete with any of the best-dressed women at the ball. She wouldn't even try.

She dressed for comfort. When she donated all of her professor clothes, she gave up ever again wearing anything that pinched, confined, or hurt.

Now every day she dressed the way she used to only on the weekends: in loose, cozy, comfortable clothes, in colors that made her feel alive.

Colors were a kind of nutrition. Bright, beautiful, uplifting to the soul.

It was why she planted flowers in the various beds surrounding her house, to drink in those colors with her eyes every day and feel her spirit brighten.

A black and white ball. Fine. She could adapt.

And she would try to buy everything she needed within twenty minutes, simply for her own amusement.

At 10:35 on the Monday after Christmas, Winnie stepped through the automatic doors of her neighborhood Target.

The interior always smelled of manufactured clothes just removed from some box, with a faint tinge of popcorn, although she could never tell why. As far as she knew, no one was serving popcorn in the store.

Although Winnie avoided shopping as much as she could, there were times when she needed to venture out to grab this or that, and she always preferred coming to Target. The lighting in the store felt right, the merchandise suited her sense of economy, and Winnie knew she could find whatever she needed in rapid time and get out, back to the quiet sanctuary of her home.

She planned her trips here for times of day when she knew there would be less of a crowd.

When Winnie was a child, she couldn't bear going to stores. Her clairvoyance flooded her with images and information, and she had no way of filtering them or shutting them off.

She could feel strangers' emotions. She knew things about them that she wished she didn't. She could see their auras, the layers of colors glowing around their bodies, and the spectacle of it always fascinated her, but it also wore her down in a very short time. She would return home so bone exhausted she would have to take to her bed for several hours.

Her parents tried to understand her. They assumed that Winnie was simply an oversensitive child. They never tried to force her into social situations they could see were too difficult for Winnie to enjoy.

She loved them for that. And it was only years later, when she really understood these gifts she had been born with, that she could explain to her parents the way her mind worked, and could express how grateful she was for their kindness all her life.

By then Winnie had begun her own experiments to test the full extent of her abilities, and how to control them. She read every book she could find about extrasensory perception, clairvoyance, and other psychic phenomena. She eventually met other clairvoyants who shared their own experiences.

By the time Winnie was in college, she had learned how to adjust her mind like turning down the volume on a TV. She could close herself off if she needed to, and stop feeling the emotions and seeing the auras of every person she passed.

But if she wanted to, she could turn it back on in a flash.

Today, though, she just wanted to zip in and out of Target with none of the extra stimulation, and buy a few pieces of clothing to get her through her date with Matthew.

From the entrance, Winnie strode straight ahead toward the women's section. She already saw something that could work.

Time was ticking away. Already a minute of her allotted twenty minutes had passed.

Winnie scooped up a plain white T-shirt folded with the other more colorful knit shirts on a set of shelves.

Next, she grabbed a one-size-fits-all glittery white knit kimono jacket modeled by a mannequin on a New Year's Eve display.

Winnie was short, just five-foot-three, so that made buying pants a challenge. But she had a sewing machine, and could make any adjustments she needed before the party.

In the sleepware section, she found soft white velvety pajama pants that tied with a drawstring at the waist. She would need to hem them, but that was no problem.

Last, shoes. Winnie checked her watch. She had eleven minutes left. Plenty of time.

She passed by the boots, the dressy flats, and anything with heels. She would never subject herself to heels again.

Her grandniece Annabelle had a pair of shoes that would be perfect if Winnie could find them in an adult size.

Maybe they weren't part of Target's normal inventory and were here only because of New Year's Eve, but Winnie found exactly what she wanted: white, glittery pull-on sneakers, the kind of thing a named designer would probably sell for hundreds of dollars to customers who wanted quirky chic.

As part of her Consumer Psychology courses, Winnie used to send her students comparison shopping at both high-end and discount stores, searching for the exact same merchandise, but sold at widely-different prices based only on the name branded on the item.

She hoped she had converted many of them to never spending more than they needed to, just for a name.

Winnie checked the price of the shoes. Perfect. She grabbed a box in her size and headed for the check out.

Out of the store in twenty minutes. Spent under fifty dollars.

A success by any definition.

While the other women at the ball would probably spend thousands of dollars to wear painful shoes and have to suck in their stomachs all night, Winnie would be wearing sneakers and pajamas.

Winnie smiled to herself as she left the store with her purchases in hand.

Now it was time to return home, fix herself another cup of coffee, and continue her research into Bradley Klader.

She wanted to know as much as she could about him before she ever came near the man.

3

———

Bradley Klader had a net worth of six hundred million dollars. Or over a billion, depending on which article you believed.

He was the founder, president, and CEO of Klader Designs, Klader Development, and Klader Construction. His development company had won the contract with Matthew's school district, and Klader Construction would soon begin building a new high school and middle school campus on the northeast side of the city to accommodate Tucson's growing population.

The man was not shy about publicity. He invited reporters to his home when he completed it a few years ago, so they could gush about how opulent and innovative it was.

Winnie lived in a 2,000-square-foot house. Bradley Klader's house was 25,000 square feet.

Winnie couldn't even imagine it. She didn't want to.

Cleaning it, alone…

Although obviously a couple as wealthy as Bradley and Bridgette Klader wouldn't spend a moment cleaning their own home.

The article listed the staff: gardener, housekeeper, cook, house manager, steward (the reporter said Klader resisted calling him a butler), and at least five other full-time workers.

Within the 25,000 square feet, the Kladers had an indoor swimming pool as well as as indoor-outdoor pool. Bridgette had been a competitive swimmer in her college years, and she wanted options for her daily workout.

Klader was a sportsman, the article said. His wing of the house included a trophy room with the taxidermied heads of some of the animals he had killed, as well as a full indoor, air-conditioned shooting range so he and his hunting pals could keep their skills sharp.

An article about one of his recent big game hunts showed a picture of Klader wearing safari khakis and grinning as he held up the limp head of a dead giraffe.

Winnie clicked off the link in disgust. She had seen enough.

While looking at the words and various photos on her computer screen, a separate stream of images had been scrolling through her mind.

Klader riding his motorcycle, helmetless, with his blond hair whipping in the wind. A scowl on his face. Something had displeased him.

Klader wearing bright orange ear protection and shooting a rifle and then a pistol. Somewhere indoors, maybe in his own shooting range.

Klader kissing a young woman with long brown hair. Klader's hand angling down her back, lower…

Klader kissing a young blonde woman. His hands working to unzip her dress…

Winnie had seen photos of Bridgette Klader, Bradley's wife. She was neither of the women he was kissing. Bridgette was in her early fifties, with bottle-blonde hair she wore in a severe asymmetric cut, to her jaw on one side, only just below her ear on the other.

Winnie could feel other images waiting to stream through her mind, but she had had enough of Bradley Klader for one day. She wanted that man out of her head.

She shut off her computer and woke Clover for a second, unscheduled walk. Winnie needed fresh air. Movement. Nature. Colors. Joy.

Clover immediately supplied the joy. The dog

wagged and panted with excitement as Winnie reached into the basket near the back door and pulled out Clover's leash.

Winnie pulled on her purple fleece vest, checking to make sure her gloves were in the pockets. She could see from the way her pomegranate tree was swaying in the back yard that the wind had come up while she worked on her computer. She didn't need to feel it for herself to have a sense of the cold. She snugged down a light blue fleece hat over her white-blonde hair, slipped on her sunglasses, and stepped out into the afternoon chill.

Clover sniffed her way along their usual route, checking to see what dogs had left her new messages since this morning.

Once they reached the university campus, Winnie unclipped Clover's leash and let the dog lead the way across the long open stretch of grass.

Not far away was Winnie's old office in the Psychology building. She had taught in that building for over thirty years.

And yet she felt a stranger to it now, as though that were a different version of her life that no longer fit.

She preferred her freedom. The lack of a schedule. No longer rushing every morning to get everything done so she could hurry to her first class on time.

She had loved teaching, and yet she didn't miss it at all.

Once Joe got sick, it had been the easiest thing in the world to retire so she could spend as much time with him as he still had.

After Joe died, friends and colleagues urged her to come back, to pick up her career again.

But that life was behind her. Winnie knew it.

On the night before he died, while already deep in a coma, Joe came to her in a vision and the two of them had one last conversation. Among other things, Joe encouraged Winnie to use her gifts in a new way. She knew he was right—he usually was.

Now Winnie was only a visitor to this campus, on her daily walks with Clover.

But normally only in the morning. Never in the afternoon, like now.

Winnie heard someone call her name.

Nothing was coincidence. She realized now that the sudden urge to walk here had hit her for a reason.

There were no classes during this week between Christmas and New Year's, but professors often came in to work for a few hours here and there, to catch up without any interruptions.

Dr. Amanda Birkauer jogged across the grass toward Winnie and Clover. Dressed in navy blue U of A athletic pants and a matching zip-up jacket, wearing running shoes and carrying a backpack, with her long brown hair in a ponytail threaded through the back of her blue

U of A baseball cap, anyone might mistake her for a student.

She was a fit and youthful looking fifty-three, fifteen years younger than Winnie, a tri-athlete in her spare time.

She, too, had a PhD in Psychology, but she used hers as the Assistant Director of the university's world-renowned mind lab research program.

For the past many years, Winnie had been one of the program's most reliable test subjects.

She had volunteered to let them study her on two conditions: that she remain anonymous, and that they share with her everything they learned.

Winnie wanted to hone her gifts in whatever ways she could. Hearing about what other clairvoyants could do helped her aim for new horizons.

"Hi!" Amanda greeted Clover, whose whole body was wagging with love.

Amanda crouched down and hugged and petted the wiggly dog, then stood up and hugged Winnie in turn.

"Stranger," Amanda said.

"I know," Winnie agreed. "I'll come do a session in a few weeks. You've been on my mind."

"You've been on mine," Amanda said. She pulled off her backpack and fished inside it. "I have something to show you. I've been meaning to call you."

Amanda pulled out an academic journal. "Italian. A

friend sent it to me, and I finally got back a translation from someone in the Languages department."

Amanda flipped through the pages of the journal to the one she had paperclipped on the side.

"I'll give you the translation with it, but the upshot is something they're calling psychic doodling ... but some Italian name for it."

Winnie chuckled. "All right."

"I won't spoil it," Amanda said, handing her the journal and a set of stapled papers Winnie assumed was the translation. "Call me after you read it. Because you're doing it next time I've got you in the lab."

Amanda crouched down in front of Clover again and gave the dog a parting hug.

"Sorry, gotta go." She gave Winnie a quick hug, too. "Happy New Year. Plans?"

Amanda was already jogging backward, so Winnie kept her answer brief.

"A ball. You?"

"Marathon."

"Of course."

Amanda blew Winnie a kiss, then turned around and took off running at her more natural pace.

Winnie smiled to herself. She had come on this errand not knowing she needed to come.

"Come on, Clove," she said, holding out the leash to clip back on Clover's collar.

The dog trotted to Winnie's side.

Winnie clutched the journal and the translation in her hand and hurried with Clover back across the grass.

There was something she needed in these papers. She was anxious to know what it was.

4

____

Problem-solving through visual representation, the Italian psychologist promised, *unlocks a portion of the psychic mind otherwise not accessible through language.*

Winnie read through the translation of the article, skimming at times, not as engaged by it as she expected to be.

She turned to the article itself where her friend Amanda had paperclipped the page. It wasn't at the beginning of the article, but about halfway through, where a black and white photograph was inset among the Italian text.

The author and three of his students—or maybe they were test subjects, Winnie couldn't read the Italian caption—sat at a long table in the middle of a small classroom or an office. The area was cramped by the long table, with barely enough room to stand between the wall and the chairs.

Winnie sensed that maybe that was the point, conducting the experiment in such a confined space.

On the table were three or four long stretches of paper, apparently created by taping together a series of blank sheets of standard-sized printer paper. Affixed to walls surrounding the table were a dozen or more of these connected pages, all of them covered with sketches, scribbles, line-drawings, and various shapes, some of them recognizable as images, but most of them not.

A young woman with dark hair sat at the table with her eyes closed, pen in hand, and appeared to be in the process of filling up one of the long stretches of blank paper with scribbles of her own. The author and the two other students, one male and one female, looked on.

Winnie could see nothing significant in what the young woman was drawing. No pattern. Nothing that seemed important. She returned to the translation of the article and skimmed ahead to where she might find a description of the photo.

Predicting an earthquake, the translation said.

Winnie looked at the girl's scribbles again. Nothing about them suggested an earthquake.

She read on.

The focusing technique of psychic doodling allowed Ms.

Testoro to accurately predict the date, time, and severity of an upcoming earthquake in the Abruzzi region of central Italy.

Interesting, but Winnie did not understand why she needed this information today. Why she felt the urge to take Clover for a walk on campus so that Amanda Birkauer could give her this article now.

Winnie sighed and closed the journal. She could feel a headache beginning in her left temple. She had done too much today, first the shopping spree, then the research into Bradley Klader, and now reading a thickly-worded academic article.

She needed sugar. Always the best remedy.

The black and white ball was just four days away now. Winnie had done enough preparation. Sometimes working too hard, pushing too hard, made it difficult for clear images and intuition to come through.

Winnie reheated in her toaster oven the last remaining cinnamon roll from Christmas. She brewed a cup of decaffeinated coffee, wanting the flavor and the warmth without the jolt.

She sat on her dark green love seat in the living room and patted the space next to her for Clover. The Lab launched herself onto the cushion and curled herself snuggly up next to Winnie.

"That Klader is a bad man," Winnie told the dog. Clover had no reaction. "But let's keep an open mind, shall we?" If Matthew wanted Winnie to give him concrete reasons not to trust Bradley Klader, it did no good to blind herself with broad, general assumptions.

But Klader was a bad man. Winnie could feel it. If she didn't have to meet him for Matthew's sake, she would want to steer clear of him for the rest of her life.

Winnie bit into her homemade cinnamon roll. It tasted like her childhood. The recipe was her mother's.

Winnie closed her eyes and leaned back against the love seat.

She purposely invited her happiest memories of being a child, hoping to erase the persistent image of Bradley Klader grinning as he held up the limp head of the giraffe he had killed.

5

Matthew showed up at the appointed hour, dressed in a black tuxedo with all the trimmings.

"You're probably too young to understand the reference," Winnie told him, "but my boy, you are Mystery Date."

"Thank you," Matthew said. "I think."

He looked over Winnie's outfit and smiled as he gave her a nod. "Perfectly you." He crooked his elbow and held out his arm for her to take. "Let's get this over with."

"Let's," Winnie agreed.

One whiff of the nighttime cold, and she briefly retreated to the house to pluck off the back of the couch a soft white throw she sometimes curled under to read a book. It was probably covered in yellow dog hair, but no one would see it in the dark, and Winnie didn't care in any case.

The Kladers' house was about forty-five minutes away, in the foothills of the Catalina mountains north of the city. At the stoplight on Skyline Road, Winnie turned to look through the back window of Matthew's Volvo to gaze at the sparkling lights of the city below.

The foothills were a beautiful area to live in, with wild desert growing around the southwestern-style mansions discreetly tucked away in gated subdivisions hidden from the road.

Matthew drove on. Bradley Klader had built his house even further north than Winnie expected.

They left pavement for a single-lane dirt road that made its winding way through the dark desert on either side. On a hill above them Winnie could see the monstrosity that was Bradley Klader's house.

It was lit up like a casino. Music reached the car, even with the windows up, at least a mile away. It must be blasting people's eardrums. Winnie wished she had thought to bring earplugs.

Her heart picked up speed. She closed her eyes and took several deep breaths.

She had long ago conquered any social anxiety, but her body still tended to go into fight-or-flight mode when it sensed the sensory overload that awaited it.

Bright, insistent colors. Too much noise. Unpleasant smells. Random thoughts and feelings of strangers trying to break into her mind.

"Are you all right?" Matthew asked.

Winnie opened her eyes and smiled. She reached over and squeezed Matthew's wrist. "Fine. I've just never enjoyed parties."

"We won't stay long," he promised. "Maybe just an hour, if you think it gives you enough time."

Winnie reminded herself of her mission. This was not a social visit. She was not a prisoner to these people. She was here to evaluate Klader for Matthew, to try to identify the source of Matthew's unease.

Winnie had her own reasons for already distrusting the man. But she needed to put that bias aside so she could see clearly—the very definition of clairvoyance.

As they rounded a bend in the road, the headlights showed the long line of parked cars that stretched into the distance.

A young man in a white uniform waved to them. Matthew slowed to a stop and the young man approached the window.

"Valet service," he told them. "We have a cart to take you the rest of the way."

He pointed behind him to a group of half a dozen golf carts waiting to ferry party guests up to the house.

Winnie wouldn't have minded walking, to clear her

head and her heart, but she followed Matthew to the foremost cart and settled in beside him behind the driver. The only sound the electric cart made as it climbed the hill came from the tires crunching stones in the dirt.

The music blared louder the higher they climbed. And unfortunately, not pretty music, but something with a loud, booming beat that drowned out whatever lyrics the band was straining to sing.

But the cold desert smelled fresh to Winnie's nose, reminding her that wild nature surrounded all these lights and noise.

One hour. She would give herself that challenge. Find Matthew's answers within the hour and then escape from this place.

The cart reached the circular driveway and drove Winnie and Matthew to the open wrought iron gates.

"Madam," the polite young cart driver said as he held out his hand to help Winnie from the cart.

She drew her soft white throw around her. A thin protection against whatever lay ahead.

6

———

The house was not a house. It was a showcase. A statement. It resembled one of the nearby resorts nestled into the foothills.

Every room was lit up to show how many rooms there were. Winnie could only imagine what the electric bill would be for tonight.

She assumed the music came from some pre-recorded selection, boomed out through multiple speakers.

But she could see a seven-piece band up on a platform, with the lead guitarist shouting into a microphone.

The drummer had no mercy. Winnie tried to pretend she was underwater and couldn't hear him.

Scores of servers circulated among what looked like a thousand guests, and those were just the ones standing outside near the tall, thin portable heaters. There were white party lights strung from a grid of thin wires above them, making strange shadows in the graveled courtyard as the people milled about.

The guests were as fancy as Rose had promised. Every man in a tuxedo, and the women in a variety of mostly black gowns. Necklines plunged to waistlines. Winnie could see more cleavage gathered in this one place than she ever needed to see the remainder of her life.

Something drew her attention. She allowed her eyes to roam.

There, to her left, at the top of a set of wide stone stairs leading to the front of the house, stood a lovely dark-haired woman in a long white gown.

She looked like a princess or a bride with pearls and diamonds dressing her swooped-up, elegant hair.

She stood with her arm twined through a tuxedoed man's arm. They both looked to be in their early thirties.

The woman's clinging white dress and her daring neckline showed off her pregnant body.

Winnie knew the woman's face, of course. She had seen it in the flash of images her mind sent her while she researched Bradley Klader.

Winnie pulled Matthew closer. She indicated the couple with a nod of her head.

"That's not her husband's child," Winnie said. "It's Klader's."

"Are you sure?" Matthew asked. Then he caught himself. "Of course you're sure."

Winnie's eyes roamed again, and she made no effort to control them.

She found the blonde woman easily, the one whose dress Klader had been unzipping in another of Winnie's flashes.

The blonde, also standing with a man who might be her husband, was also, improbably, pregnant.

Winnie sighed and subtly pointed her out. "That one, too."

"You're kidding," Matthew said.

"There might even be others, but those were the only two I saw."

Now, curious, Winnie took control of her gaze again and searched for the party's hostess, Bridgette Klader.

But neither of the Kladers seemed to be out here in the cold. They must be inside with a whole other set of guests.

"Thank God," said a man behind them.

Winnie knew that voice. She turned, already smiling.

"Troy." She opened her arms and welcomed him

into a hug. Troy Vargas was at least a foot taller than she was. He had to bend down to complete the embrace.

"Aunt Win," he said. "You have made my night."

"Look at you," she said. "Handsome as ever." With his charm and good looks, he always reminded her of a young Denzel Washington.

Troy and Matthew did the slapping, complicated handshake that some young men do, especially if they've known each other a long time.

"Where's Rosie?" Troy asked.

"Home with Annabelle," Matthew said.

"Well, can't complain if you brought Win instead."

Troy had been part of Rose's study group in law school. Winnie fed all five of those kids more meals than she could remember over the course of their three years of school.

The last time Winnie saw Troy was at Joe's funeral. She had been touched that all of the study group came.

"What are you doing here?" Matthew asked him.

"Hustling for the firm," said Troy. "Lot of movers and shakers here tonight. Potential future clients. But what you have to learn is how to tell the truly rich from the wannabes."

"Educate me," Winnie said. Aside from her niece, she had always liked Troy best of the group. She enjoyed hearing his opinions and theories while the kids studied. Troy was the most creative of all of them about how to argue cases.

"Rich people wear comfortable shoes," Troy said. "Like you," he told Winnie, pointing to her sneakers. "Not like you," he smirked at Matthew, "standing there in your shiny rental shoes."

"You're saying you own that?" Matthew asked, pointing at Troy's tux.

"Have we just met?" Troy said. "You think I want to wear this more than once?"

A server came by, carrying a tray of appetizers. Some sort of meat and cheese on top of a square of crispy bread.

"Don't do that," Troy warned Matthew, who was reaching for a square. "Excuse me," Troy asked the young woman carrying the tray. "What is that?"

"Bear," she said.

"Uh-huh, no thank you." Troy kindly moved her along. "I got a mouthful of rattlesnake a little while ago," he told Winnie and Matthew. "The guy can't just serve regular food. There's probably a tray of bunny intestines somewhere around here. As soon as this is over I'm going to grab a pizza."

Winnie had to resist the urge to hug him again. She had missed this wonderful man.

"So. Rich people," she reminded him.

"Right," Troy said. "They like *tailored*." He pointed to

a man off to their right who had a noticeably large belly. "Look how those buttons are straining." Troy groaned. "The guy's sweating. Can't breathe. He'll be flat out on the ground pretty soon. Should've skipped the *bear*, sir. Not very slimming. Too bad."

"Whereas *that* one," Troy continued, indicating an even heavier man to their left. "Rich. Fat and rich. See the difference?"

Winnie could. The man's clothes fit him properly. He didn't try to hide his girth, he just paid for a tuxedo that accommodated it.

"Another thing," Troy said, still enriching Winnie's base of knowledge. "There's rich, and then there's private plane rich. And then there's renting a private plane versus owning one."

"Which is Bradley Klader?" Winnie asked.

"Oh, he owns two. His and hers so they can both do their own thing."

Winnie glanced again at the pregnant brunette.

She wondered if Mrs. Klader knew about the two pregnant mistresses. Or if she cared.

The band paused in its auditory assault. A new voice took control of the microphone.

"Welcome, ladies and gentleman," the man said. "If you haven't bid in the silent auction yet, you have about one hour. And remember, all proceeds benefit the Klader Children's Charities, so open your wallets, ___s!"

The last word was not one Winnie expected to hear in such expensive company. But the crowd cheered like they were at a football game.

"Klader," Troy said. "Classy, huh? But you don't have to be if you own the whole state."

Winnie strained to see the man standing on the band's platform. Klader, all right. She recognized his stocky frame and the unflattering shade of his yellow hair.

Clover's fur was more attractive. Winnie had samples of it on the throw around her shoulders is anyone wanted her to prove it.

"What do you know about him?" Matthew asked. Winnie was glad he did. Troy worked for one of the larger law firms in town. He moved in circles Winnie never would.

"Slow rise," Troy said, "but now he's one of the top dogs. He's got developments all over the Southwest. Even built one of the casinos in Vegas."

Winnie smiled to herself. She had been right about the look of the house.

"That deal he made with your district is small fry," Troy said. "No offense, but I'm surprised he's bothering."

"It's the biggest contract we've ever given," Matthew said.

Troy shrugged. "Like I said, no offense."

"Then why would he?" Winnie asked. "Make the deal."

"Maybe throw some work to one of his subs," Troy guessed. "Give them something to do in between bigger jobs. Or just because the guy likes to see his name everywhere. Maybe he drives by that way every day and wants a thrill."

Those didn't sound like good reasons to Winnie. But she didn't have any ideas of her own.

"What do you know about him personally?" Winnie asked. She had already read several profiles of Klader, and knew the basics of his background. But she wondered if Troy had heard more.

"Ex-college wrestler," he said. "One of the California schools, I think USC. Met the fine Missus when she was a superstar swimmer there. One daughter, named *Moxie,* if you can stand it. Still in college, I think. She's probably wandering around here somewhere."

"How are they as a couple?" Winnie asked. It probably had nothing to do with Matthew's contract with Klader, but she was curious just the same.

Troy laughed. "Uh ... volcano and spinning knives? Acid and flaming gasoline? Not very pleasant when they're together. But they've built a hell of an empire. Must work for them somehow."

"Is he ... honest?" Winnie asked.

Troy hooted. "Oh, Aunt Win. You slay me."

"Anything you can prove?" Matthew asked.

Troy held up his hands in surrender. "Hey, I'm just here to not eat rattlesnake and hand out some business cards. I in no way vouch for our host. I think he's sleazy as hell."

Winnie and Matthew exchanged a glance.

It was time for her to stop socializing, and time to get to work.

7

During her time as a test subject for the mind lab, Winnie had met other clairvoyants.

She was always interested in hearing from them how they managed the challenges of everyday life.

How they filtered out the noise, the lights, the information.

Her best advice had come from a woman named Mae.

Mae sat with Winnie in one of the small rooms of the lab and guided her in a special meditation.

Winnie learned to see her gifts as settings on different dials. If she concentrated on quieting her mind, she could consciously turn them up or down as she wished.

Now, standing in the courtyard outside Bradley

Klader's house, Winnie closed her eyes and calmed her mind.

Troy had reluctantly excused himself for a while to go mingle with potential clients.

The band was taking a break, but equally unpleasant music blared from the speakers on the stage.

Winnie closed her mind to distractions and opened it to her greater awareness.

She visualized the dial corresponding to her ability to see auras, and she turned it up to 8. Before the party, she had set it to 1.

She moved to the next dial, psychic insight, and turned it up to 10.

Dial by dial, she adjusted her mental settings, until she felt comfortable and properly balanced. She breathed deeply a few more times with her eyes still closed, then opened them and looked up at Matthew.

"All right," she said, taking Matthew's arm. "Let's go inside and see what we see."

The crowd around them looked different now. Winnie could see auras glowing around every body.

She concentrated on walking forward, trying not to notice the energy fields of all these random strangers. But she kept that sight open, waiting to see certain specific people. Her first impression of their auras would be the most vivid. She didn't want to have to turn on the ability too late.

She had already seen Klader up on the platform when he made his announcement about the silent auction, but after a brief glance, she purposely looked away.

To her left were the pregnant brunette mistress and her husband. The woman's aura was a mishmash of neon green, an unpleasant yellow, and a film of gray overlaying them both.

Different clairvoyants saw different colors, Winnie had learned. Mae might look at the mistress and see her all in red.

It was as individual as someone's sense of taste and smell. Winnie had made a catalog of aura colors over the years, deciphering her own personal color code.

But one thing that seemed to be true for them all was that black showed a tendency to darkness. Black was the aura of liars and thieves. Of people who committed violence. A black aura was a warning. Black was the aura of evil.

Winnie had seen it in her life, more times than she ever wanted.

But she valued the information. She trusted her mind to keep her safe.

The host of the black and white ball stood in the opulent front entrance hall of his house, and Winnie could barely see his face past the fog of black.

She paused and looked down at her glittery white

sneakers. Then she looked up again to see if the image had changed.

It had, in that she saw a quick flash of an image. Too fast for her to see what it was.

But the *feeling*. The sense of dread in her heart. Whatever that image had been, it had made her pulse quicken.

Klader looked up then, and noticed Matthew. For a moment Klader frowned, as if trying to place him.

Then he smiled and strode away from the people he'd been entertaining, and came at Matthew with his hand outstretched.

"Matt! Good to see you!" Klader looked at Winnie and seemed confused. "Where's your beautiful wife?"

"Home with our sick daughter," Matthew lied smoothly. "This is her aunt, Mrs. Parsons."

Winnie had suggested he introduce her as *Mrs.* rather than *Doctor*. Doctor might be too memorable. And Winnie didn't want to be remembered.

She had traded her black plastic framed glasses for the thin wire frames that drew less attention to her face. She wore no makeup. She had no need to impress anyone. To the contrary, the dowdier and frumpier she appeared, the better.

Old people tended to disappear into the background. Winnie liked to use that to her advantage.

Movement to her right drew Winnie's eyes. Here was the woman she recognized from the online articles.

Bridgette Klader looked exactly like her photos. Although her strong features could be viewed as attractive, her jagged, asymmetric haircut framed her face in an unflattering way.

She joined her husband now to meet these strangers who had dared to enter her house. Bridgette stood taller than her husband by several inches. Winnie guessed she might even be six feet tall. Added to that, Mrs. Klader wore excessively high heels that raised her even higher. She towered over her ex-wrestler husband.

Her whole body was bathed in a pulsating black cloud. When she stood next to Klader, the two auras seemed to unite.

Winnie had seen enough. And being this close to them was making her heart speed. She dropped her gaze to the travertine tiles on the floor and spared them having to look any longer at the Kladers.

"Bridge," Klader said to his wife, "this is Matt Mason, head of the school district."

From the corner of her eye, Winnie could see the two of them shake hands.

"And who's this?" Bridgette Klader asked Matthew.

"My wife's aunt," Matthew said. "My wife is sick..." Winnie could hear the nervousness in his voice. A woman like Bridgette Klader could be intimidating.

Winnie didn't blame Matthew for feeling uncomfortable.

"Ah, last minute," Mrs. Klader said. "That explains it. It's so hard to find proper clothes on such short notice."

Winnie raised her eyes. She couldn't help the smile that teased her lips. She had known women like Bridgette Klader all of her life. She was as immune to their snotty, snobby comments as she was to anyone who doubted the reality of her gifts.

Winnie knew in her bones who she was. She knew who she loved and who loved her. She knew the strength of her mind and the quality of her heart. Bridgette Klader's opinion meant less than nothing.

Winnie was here to do a job for Matthew. She had seen what she needed to see, and now she could go.

Two pregnant mistresses. This garish house. The black auras around both of the Kladers.

Anything else, Winnie would find out in other ways. Her gifts would show her what she needed to know.

"I'm afraid I'm not feeling well," Winnie told Matthew. "Would you take me home?"

"Oh ... of course," Matthew said. He seemed surprised. But he said goodbye to their hosts and then led her out.

Winnie did not say goodbye. She said nothing to them at all. They didn't deserve her words.

As soon as they were back outside, Winnie said, "What horrible people."

"Did you get anything?" Matthew asked. "Any … feeling?"

"You were right to be worried," Winnie said. "I don't know all the reasons why, but I'm still working on it. Give me time."

They found Troy before they left.

"I'm starving," he said. "Pizza?"

"Nah, I should get home," Matthew said.

"I'll invite you for dinner soon," Winnie said. "With Rose and Matthew. Will you come?"

Troy leaned down and kissed Winnie on the cheek. "Aunt Win, just try to keep me away."

Winnie was about to go, but then decided Troy might be able to help her. Although she was the one with a Doctorate in Psychology, Troy seemed to have a special understanding of the ways of the rich.

"I wonder," Winnie said, "what drives a man like Bradley Klader? Why build this ridiculous house? Why compete for the contract on Matthew's schools, if he doesn't need the money?"

Why have two mistresses? But Winnie kept that to herself. She didn't want to fuel any gossip.

"Why does he have a shooting range and a trophy room in his house?" Winnie asked. "Who needs to kill an innocent giraffe to feel like a big man?"

"Giraffe?" Troy said with disgust. "God, I hope he's not serving that tonight. I don't know anything about hunting—that's just never been my thing—but the rest of your question is easy.

"Once you reach a certain level," he said, "it's all just a way of keeping score. Klader doesn't need another dime, but he likes to win."

Winnie stood in the cold air, under the strings of white light in the courtyard. She breathed in the fresh scent of the winter desert.

What Troy said had the ring of truth. But it couldn't be the full answer.

"And what about Mrs. Klader? Does she need to win, too?"

Troy laughed. "It's a whole sick culture up here. The games these people play with each other. I guarantee there are at least fifty people here tonight who hate Klader's guts and wish he would die. But they get something from knowing him. So yeah, they'll show up here and open their wallets, just like he said, and they'll give money everyone pretends is going to some charity."

"It's not?" Winnie asked.

"The charity of Bradley and Bridgette Klader," Troy said. "How else do they pay for planes and safaris and Bridgette's not-so-tiny drug habit? Or for Klader's gambling life in Vegas? And who's going to pay for all the little babies he keeps having with his buddies' wives?"

"You know about that?" Winnie asked.

"Do *you*?" Troy said with surprise.

"I might have heard something," Winnie said.

"Yeah, well forget it," said Troy. "I'm sorry about most of the stuff I know."

Winnie could see the light surrounding Troy. A pale green aura around his head, a light purple around his chest. Light purple for a kind and generous heart.

He had been a good young man, a good friend for Rose. And he was still a good man. Winnie was glad to see it.

But her head was starting to hurt. The noise and lights were just too much. And she still didn't have the full truth of Bradley Klader to offer Matthew.

But maybe she was closer, thanks to Troy.

Winnie tugged at the lapel of his tuxedo and pulled him down so she could kiss his cheek.

She could smell a faint trace of aftershave on his face.

"Happy New Year," she said.

"Yeah, to both of you," Troy answered. He and Matthew did their special handshake again, and then Troy waded back into the crowd.

8

____

On the drive home, Winnie could feel the headache building in her skull. Being so close to evil had its effect.

She wasn't sure what she expected to learn tonight. But it felt important to see the Kladers in person.

"How much proof do you need if you want to cancel your contract with Klader?" Winnie asked. "Because we already know the man is poison."

"I can't just say I don't like him—"

"Or trust him," Winnie added.

"I can't back out unless I have a legal reason. There are penalties for breaching the contract. I can't subject the district to that just because I changed my mind about doing business with him."

"All right," Winnie said. "Give me a few more days.

But there's no question in my mind you shouldn't have anything to do with him."

"I don't think anybody is absolutely clean these days," Matthew said. "Maybe none of the other developers are any better."

"Maybe," Winnie said. "But I only know about this one so far. I'm going to do everything I can to help you."

Clover was asleep on the couch when Winnie returned. She thumped her tail once when Winnie sank down beside her.

It was ten minutes past midnight. "Happy New Year," Winnie told the dog.

She changed out of her party clothes and took a hot shower, hoping to wash the black stench of the Kladers away.

She changed into a nightgown and slid between the flannel sheets on her bed.

She hesitated, but in the end knew what she should do. She returned to the dials within her mind.

Maximum clarity. Maximum insight and intuition. Maximum foresight, if her mind wanted to give it.

Winnie's ability to see the future had always been sporadic. She felt as though she were still wearing training wheels on that skill. It was one of the things she tried to work on in the university's mind lab. But there always seemed to be barriers to it in her mind.

"Show me," she told herself as she drifted off to sleep.

But in the morning she knew nothing more than the night before.

She fixed herself coffee that she drank from a San Francisco mug. She had already put away Joe's Santa mug until the next Christmas.

She brought her coffee back to bed. Clover was still sleeping on top of the covers. She wouldn't get up until Winnie finished her coffee and was ready for their walk.

This small cozy home was such a contrast from the mansion where she'd been last night. She couldn't imagine waking in a monstrosity like that.

Her thoughts drifted to Bridgette Klader again. To the hardness of her eyes. To the harshness of her face.

Drug habit, Troy had said. Winnie believed it.

Everything about that woman seemed hard and wrong.

But Bradley Klader was worse. Even if Winnie didn't know every detail about the man, she still knew more than enough to want Matthew to get away.

The two pregnant mistresses. And maybe more than those two.

Stealing money from their friends, pretending it was going to a charity.

Once you reach a certain level, it's a way of keeping score.

Klader doesn't need another dime, but he likes to win.

An image flashed into Winnie's mind.

The photo from the Italian journal.

Why that? Why now?

But she saw it again. The woman sitting at the table in that tiny room.

Winnie set her mug on the bedside table and went to her office to retrieve the journal.

She brought it back to bed and snuggled under the covers, then flipped to the page that Amanda Birkauer had paperclipped.

Winnie stared at the black and white photo. She waited for her mind to offer more information.

Something about the long stretch of papers on the table appealed to her. All that space to just draw and write.

"Is that it?" Winnie asked out loud.

Then she waited to feel the answer.

She saw herself taping together two sheets of printer paper.

Winnie got out of bed and pulled on her robe.

Her kitchen table was round and seated only four. It wouldn't be big enough for this task.

But she had a long rectangular folding table in her back room that she kept for when the whole family came to dinner.

Clover followed Winnie into the living room.

"Not yet," Winnie told her, and she pointed to the couch.

Clover launched herself onto the cushions and settled back down to sleep until Winnie was ready.

Winnie set up the table in the living room. Then she picked up a stack of printer paper and a roll of tape.

Not knowing what might come of it, she obeyed the prompting in her mind. She taped together a long stretch of papers that filled the length of the table.

She looked at the picture in the Italian journal again. The woman held what looked like a Sharpie.

Winnie had a variety of those in different colors. She chose a dark gray that would show up well on the page.

The translation of the article had called it psychic doodling, and described the method.

Let the mind drift. Don't try to direct the pen. Don't even watch it. Just let the hand draw what it wanted to draw.

It reminded Winnie of something called free writing. Letting the hand write continuously for a set length of time, without trying to control or even notice what words were appearing on the page.

The Italian woman in the experiment had used psychic doodling to predict the next major earthquake. By the end of all her scribbling, she knew the exact date and time and place.

Those facts had proven accurate. The earthquake appeared just when she said.

Maybe this was a way for Winnie to bypass the barriers in her mind that kept her from clearly seeing the future.

She set her chair at the left end of the table and picked up the gray Sharpie and began.

It was strange at first, trying not notice her hand. Winnie looked at the wall in front of her. She looked out the window.

She listened to the soft rhythmic sound of Clover's snoring. She closed her eyes and tried not to think.

While her eyes were closed her hand continued to move. She could feel it making shapes, mostly circles and lines.

She stood from her chair so she could keep moving along the table. Winnie let her hand decide the pace and where it wanted to go.

Images began streaming through her mind. Bradley Klader striding through what looked like a casino.

Klader kissing yet another woman.

Klader shaking hands with two well-dressed men outside what looked like a warehouse.

A computer screen, with too much information scrolling by for Winnie to read any individual words.

Her hand was drawing faster now. Winnie moved to her right so it could keep on drawing.

She had no sense of how much time had passed when at last her pen slipped from the right edge of the table. Winnie opened her eyes. She had filled every sheet of paper.

She stepped back and surveyed what she had made.

She had drawn mostly arrows. Some thin, some thick. She counted twelve of them in all. Arrows followed by circles, by scribbled sketches, then by more circles and arrows.

She didn't realize she had written any words, but in one circle she wrote HERE and in another wrote THIS.

There were numbers below certain arrows.

Winnie felt a fluttery lightness. It was as though she had left her own body for a while and came to this table to write herself some clues.

But they were only clues, not the answers. Winnie stared at the scribbles with growing frustration.

Then one of the strange sketches caught her eye. A half circle on the left, and a jagged set of lines completing it on the right.

The longer Winnie stared at it, the more it came to resemble a mouth.

A round, ravenous, open mouth, gobbling a collection of little dots Winnie had made with her pen.

Then an arrow. And another gobbling mouth.

A circle with the word THIS.

Then the vision came upon her so suddenly, Winnie sank onto the floor for her own safety.

She saw Bradley Klader, but different now. His blond hair had grown slightly longer.

He sat in the trophy room of his mansion, surrounded by the heads of the beautiful animals he had killed.

His legs were splayed out in front of him. He slouched in a wide leather chair. His face looked slack. Winnie could see the man's despair.

Bradley took a drink from the tumbler he held in his left hand.

Then with his right he raised a pistol and shot himself in the head.

The scene skipped backward. Winnie saw Klader talking to the two men in front of the warehouse.

Then the scene skipped again. Klader walking through a casino.

HERE the vision flashed, in Winnie's handwriting from the page.

Then five numbers, then the word THIS.

Winnie's eyes flew open. She pressed her hand to her chest. Her heart was thumping. She sat where she was and caught her breath.

Then she quickly rose to her feet and picked up the gray Sharpie again. She made herself notes before she forgot any of the vision.

The black and white ball probably lasted well into the morning. The Kladers would probably sleep in until close to noon.

Winnie dressed warmly and took Clover for her walk.

All the while sorting through the information swirling through her head.

She would go see Bradley Klader today.

Just the thought of it made her feel sick.

But it was the only way to solve this.

Her mind had told her the truth.

9

Winnie dressed in comfortable clothes. Soft stretchy pants, a peach-colored fleece sweater over a white T-shirt.

Matthew had tried to talk her out of what she wanted to do, but Rose convinced him to trust that Winnie was right.

He called ahead to make sure that Klader would meet with them at his house. Matthew picked up Winnie in the Volvo and drove north again.

She gazed out the window at the desert landscape passing by. The low winter sunlight washed out the colors of the plants, making them look gray and stark and dry.

Winnie felt a different kind of dread than last night.

But she also knew now what she knew.

She rewrote her notes in a neater hand. She glanced at them again, to look at the date.

Five numbers: a day, a month, and a year.

The day that Bradley Klader would shoot himself in the head.

A woman answered the door. She wore a uniform that identified her as staff.

She led Winnie and Matthew across the front entryway, further into the house than they had ventured last night.

Klader sat behind an imposingly large desk. His eyes looked bloodshot. He didn't look well.

But he smiled at both of them in an ugly, arrogant way.

Winnie wanted to keep their meeting as brief as possible.

She and Matthew sat in the two chairs on the opposite side of the desk. Klader peered at them and waited.

Winnie said, "You have a meeting next week with two men in Las Vegas. Their names are Chapman and Morris."

Klader's bloodshot eyes slightly widened. He stared at Winnie and waited for her to say more.

"You have a mistress there. Her named is Heather. She lives in an apartment you pay for." Winnie told Klader the address.

Klader suddenly exploded. "Who are you? What do

you want?" He turned on Matthew. "What is this? Some kind of shakedown?"

Winnie calmly referred to her notes. "You've sold certain data to Chapman and Morris. That's your business, isn't it? Selling data?"

Klader's face burned red. His bloodshot eyes glared at Winnie.

"That's why you want the school district development," Winnie said. "Once it's done, you also install the computer network."

She had seen it in her vision, but Matthew also confirmed it from their contract. That was part of the Klader Development deal.

"You sell names, social security numbers, birthdates, all sorts of other data. From every job you do."

Klader's eyes had lost some of their intensity. But he still watched Winnie with a wariness that confirmed she was right to come at him this way.

"But it's about to go all wrong," Winnie said. "Sooner than you think." She held up the paper with her notes. "By August fifteenth of this year you're going to be sitting alone in your trophy room, and you're going to shoot yourself in the head."

Klader spat out a curse. Winnie didn't flinch. She knew it was hard to hear of one's death.

"I can tell you exactly what to do to avoid it. I saw it in a vision this morning."

Klader cursed again, but then he shifted in his chair. Winnie knew that kind of movement. It was a sign that a person was unsure.

"I will tell you everything I saw," Winnie said. "But first you're going to cancel your contract with the school district."

Matthew had prepared an agreement, on Winnie's suggestion. He now slid it across Klader's desk.

Klader pinched his bottom lip between his fingers and stared at the document in front of him.

"Your hair will be different," Winnie said. "Slightly longer. Have you decided to grow it out? Maybe Heather likes it better that way."

"Shut up."

"I've helped other people change their futures, too."

Klader looked up again and stared across the desk at Winnie. She could smell the rancid sweat leaking from his skin. It was the kind of sweat the body made when it was under extreme stress. Winnie stared back with patient green eyes.

She had thought about what to say to this man. How hard to push him. What he might do.

If he made their deal, it wouldn't change him. It would only change the date of his death.

Years ago Winnie attended a lecture by a psychologist who specialized in ethics. The title of his talk was *Understanding the Ethics of Evil.*

He said that people misunderstand the function of a conscience. It isn't meant to make us be good, it's only there to show us when we fall short of living our values. It is there to act as a compass, to direct us back onto our natural path.

Someone who values power at any cost will view deception as a legitimate way to win. They believe it means they are smart.

Someone who values domination over others will see cruelty as a strength. They believe that being kind means they are weak.

We may view their behavior as evil, but these people will never feel guilty for what they do.

They are acting in complete alignment with their values. Their compass tells them they are on their right path.

A man like Klader lived from a set of values so vastly different from Winnie's, it would be no use for her to try to make him change. He wouldn't feel guilty about any of the wicked things he did, because to him, they weren't wicked.

Klader was a man of appetites. He did what he wanted to satisfy them.

He saw himself as a winner. He was clever. Smarter than anyone else.

He got away with the kinds of things that Winnie couldn't imagine ever wanting to do. Her conscience would stop her at the very first step. She couldn't be like Klader for even an hour.

But she could save Matthew from having to do business with the man, and she could save Matthew from the crime Klader would commit at the end of the project.

If it meant telling Klader the date when he would put a bullet in his head, then that was an easy price to pay.

Because Winnie could warn Klader this time. But he was on the path to ruin nonetheless.

He would still lie. He would cheat. He would steal. He would pursue power at any cost.

And if he survived August fifteenth of this year, another day just like it would still be coming in his future.

Klader swore at them both, but he signed Matthew's agreement. Then he held out his hand for Winnie's notes.

She had laid it all out for him: the scenes she saw that led to that final crisis. She let Klader read it, and she waited to answer his questions.

But he only had one. "This is for real?"

"Yes," Winnie said. "I'm a psychic."

"What am I thinking right now?" Klader asked.

"I only see your future," Winnie said. But anyone could have guessed what the man was thinking.

Winnie stood from her chair, signaling that the meeting was over. Matthew reached for the signed agreement and followed Winnie to the door.

She looked back briefly and saw Klader staring at her notes. She closed the door behind her and then continued out of the house.

She took Matthew's arm, just as she did the night before. She could see Klader's signature on the document Matthew held.

Matthew swiped his free hand across his forehead. Despite the mild temperature, the poor man was sweating.

Winnie patted his arm. "Maybe next time I should meet the person ahead of time," she said. "It might save us a lot of trouble."

Matthew said nothing until he had driven them out of sight of the house. Then he braked to a stop and turned to Winnie.

"I cannot believe you just did that," he said. He leaned over and kissed her on the cheek and said, "Thank you."

Then with a sigh of relief he set the car in motion again and drove them away from that horrible place.

A DROP OF SWEAT

Winnie sat in the narrow inner courtyard between her front gate and her front door. The pathway between the planting beds was hard brick, but she always brought a soft, plush pillow with her to sit on. She was past the days of ever subjecting herself to discomfort if she could help it.

The pillow was actually a dog bed that Clover her yellow Labrador had rejected within a day of Winnie bringing it home. Something about the shallow sides, or maybe the texture of the corduroy fabric along the rim … Clover was a girl of strong opinions, and Winnie had no desire to try to boss her.

They lived as companions and roommates, both admiring and respecting each other. Clover especially admired Winnie's ability to toss cubes of cheese and slices of carrots into the air when she was cooking. Every evening Clover sat diligently on the long blue runner rug in the kitchen between the sink and the stove while Winnie cooked dinner, waiting for that magic toss.

But now, midmorning, after their walk from the house to the University of Arizona campus where they always completed the same three-mile loop, and after their respective breakfasts of kibble and oatmeal and coffee, Winnie sat on the rejected dog bed and Clover lay sleeping on the brick pathway in the sun, and they breathed in the fresh, flower-scented air and thought their own deep thoughts.

Even in January, Winnie's flower garden prospered. She no longer spoke to the plants out loud, ever since her neighbor to the south had built an extension onto her house that brought her patio right up against Winnie's tall stucco wall—the woman was an ortho-pedic surgeon at the university hospital, and had proven herself nosy and judgmental almost immediately after moving in—but Winnie still spoke in her mind to the courtyard's climbing sweet peas and bougainvillea, complimenting them on their stunning purple and magenta blossoms, and thanking them for their beauty.

She grew daisies here, too, and hollyhocks, pansies, and petunias. On the other side of the house, where the sun shone longer throughout the day, she grew fruit trees and vegetables and tall, cheerful-looking sunflowers that poked their heads above the wall.

Winnie needed color in her life, and sometimes the desert landscape of Tucson felt too brown and drab and dry.

Winnie favored life. It was the simplest thing in the world to surround herself with evidence of it inside the wall surrounding her modest, comfortable home, when outside this wall the world sometimes wanted to show her a much darker picture.

That was on her mind this morning, the ugliness of some people. She had received an email from her friend Dr. Amanda Birkauer, Assistant Director of the U of A's mind lab—also known as the parapsychology research program—telling Winnie of a nasty surprise one of her colleagues had come home to the day before.

Greetings, love. I'm forwarding an email I got from
Dr. Benjamin Rook, an old grad school pal of mine.
He lives like a hermit in the Colorado mountains,
which is why this whole thing is so weird.

His specialty is fairly new, Plant Neurobiology—a
VERY controversial field. Issue is whether plants are
more like animals and have their own version of a
brain and nervous system. Too long to go into here,
but trust me, absolutely fascinating. But I'm not

*kidding, fist fights have broken out over it. At confer-
ences, between botanists! Picture that.*

Anyway.

*Ben's problem seems like something you might be
able to help him with. Let me know. If you're game
for it and want the case, I'll give him your contact
info. But I didn't want to do that unless you say so.*

Take care! And as you'll see, poor Benjamin!

Xo

Then followed a copy of the email from Dr.
Benjamin Rook to Amanda Birkauer.

Amanda—

Well, it finally happened to me.

*I knew other people sometimes had problems at their
labs, but up here? That had to take real planning.
And a special level of hate.*

*I just got back from a conference in Frankfurt. Lots
of anger, no surprise. Actual booing while I read my*

paper. Then the discussion afterwards—Colosseum-like blood thirst. Crowd mostly cheering for the lions.

I expected it, but still. You keep hoping, right? But some of the old guard just won't bend.

Happy to get on the plane and come back here to the peace and solitude.

Except, horror show.

I have no idea when, but sometime in the past ten days someone broke into my house and the lab and trashed EVERYTHING. No exaggeration, ALL OF IT.

My clothing, my furniture, my food, my gear, and stupid, pointless stuff like unrolling all my toilet paper and stomping it onto the floor with dirty boots. Plugging the toilet with rags so it would overflow. Propping the freezer lid open to spoil everything. Just asinine stuff like that. If they weren't hibernating, bears would have come for miles to feast on this place.

But that was just the house. Horrible enough. But the

LAB. Don't mind telling you, I cried like a child when I saw it.

Fifteen years of work, Amanda. All that money, but worse, all that TIME.

And I know you probably don't understand, but I was mostly crying for the plants.

I had about 300 of them in there. Different species, special hybrids, various cooperative communities I've been developing over the years. My own specially-designed ecosystem.

Whoever did it didn't just turn off the watering system or pull the plants out by their roots.

They MASSACRED them. Smashed every pot. Ripped apart every plant leaf by leaf, stem by stem. Stomped every fruit and vegetable. Stabbed into the bulbs. Took the time to kill every one of them individually, not just a smash and go.

WHY? There was no reason. It was gratuitous. Just a Screw You to me. To make sure I couldn't just pull out a broom and sweep up all the damage and start again in a few days.

Starting over—if I do it, and that's a BIG if right now, Amanda, I'm being honest—will set me back years. First the funding—if ever. That's already been next to impossible most of the time. Then reproducing all the equipment. You know how long it took me to make all of it. So much of it was just trial and error. What if I can't recreate that magic?

I don't know, I'm probably just rambling now. It's been several hours since I came home to all this, and I'm still shaken.

Yes, I called the sheriff. No, I don't have any security cameras up here. Electricity and connectivity are already a challenge. I save it all for the lab.

I'm mentally DONE right now. I'm sending this to you because (a) you are a problem-solver. I need that. And (b) your ideas are usually so crazy-brilliant, I wouldn't be able to come up with anything close to them on my own.

If you say, I got nothing, Ben, good luck to you—I'll hate it, but I'll understand. I won't hate you.

And no, I have no idea who did this. The Frankfurt kind of people are big talkers/yellers, but it's taking it to a whole other level to actually drive up here in the winter, trek from the road all the way out to this place (no ski tracks or snow shoe tracks—I looked), and then really commit to being the kind of violent lunatic you'd have to be to do what they did.

Any help appreciated. No idea too radical. I'm just wrung out. Going to finally go to bed now. See if this all turns out to be a dream.

Thanks.
—Ben

Winnie was no stranger to the kind of hatred Benjamin Rook described. At sixty-eight, Dr. Winifred Parsons, retired psychology professor, an esteemed scholar in the field of Consumer Psychology, had hidden her true gifts from most of her colleagues during her nearly forty years teaching at the university.

She knew that not everyone would embrace her extraordinary talents: clairvoyance, medical intuition, and occasional foresight into the future.

She volunteered as Test Subject Number 2143 in Amanda Birkauer's parapsychology research lab—also known as the mind lab—at the university. Winnie wanted to add to the body of knowledge about psi abilities, and also wanted to learn more about it herself.

She volunteered after being assured that her participation would be kept a secret.

But she also knew that for some people, keeping a secret meant you only told one person at a time. Winnie trusted Amanda Birkauer, but she didn't trust everyone. She already learned that lesson when she was young.

One Sunday morning, when Winnie was ten, the pastor of her family's church gave a special sermon. It was about the evils of sorcery and divination—probably the same kind of sermon given years later when a certain series of books about a boy wizard took the world by storm—and Winnie had been only half listening when suddenly she heard her own name.

The pastor pointed to where Winnie sat with her parents and her brother Steven, and called Winnie an instrument of the devil. A danger to the other children. Winnie's mother reached over and gripped her hand so hard, Winnie could feel her knuckles pop.

Winnie realized in that moment that she had made a mistake. A few days before she had finally revealed to her friend Marsha, who went to the same church, that she could see colors all around Marsha's body, and that she could see them around everybody else, too.

Marsha seemed scared, but also thrilled. She asked Winnie what else she could see.

Winnie told her about a recent prophetic dream. She

knew that the school bus driver was going to have a heart attack the day before he did.

And then—and Winnie knew in her heart she was showing off now, but Marsha kept asking her for more and more—Winnie said that she could see inside Marsha's body, and saw something dark purple and gooey inside Marsha's intestines. She said it didn't look right.

Marsha started crying then. She told Winnie to take it back. But Winnie knew she had told the truth.

Even though it was supposed to be their secret, Marsha must have told her parents. And then they told the pastor...

And by Sunday the sermon was tailored especially for the devil-worshipper in their midst.

There had been other lessons after that, not all of them as painful or public, but Winnie learned to keep her knowledge to herself.

Even if that knowledge might help someone. Sometimes the risk was too high.

But Winnie was older now. She no longer had a professional reputation to protect. And the urge to be able to help people with her gifts had finally overcome her resistance to exposure.

But the final, gentle push had come from her husband Joe the night before he died. After that, Winnie set off on a new path.

But she still protected herself by only taking cases referred to her by people she trusted.

Amanda Birkauer was right to think that Winnie would want to help Dr. Benjamin Rook.

And that Winnie's gifts might be exactly what he needed—even though now, sitting here in the beautiful morning light among her olive trees and flowers, she didn't have a single idea about what to do.

Winnie's morning meditation was over. Her mind had chattered to her the whole time. She wouldn't have any peace until she wrote back to Amanda.

She rose and picked up Clover's rejected dog bed. Clover herself stood and yawned and stretched in the sun. Then the dog followed Winnie into the house, to Winnie's office.

Amanda, Winnie replied to the email. *Yes, send him my way. Tell him my background and about my fees. No surprises.*

If not for her years studying the field of Consumer Psychology, Winnie might have felt tempted to take Benjamin Rook's case for free. It was not the first time she had felt that way.

But she knew that her clients would place a greater value—and trust—in her advice if they paid handsomely for it. It was a strange fact of human nature. Winnie wanted to make sure her clients did not look upon her as some fortune teller from a carnival who would tell them their future for a dollar. She was a professional who took herself and her gifts seriously.

Winnie sent the email to Amanda, then opened a fresh window on her computer to begin her research.

Plant Neurobiology. She would see what all the fuss was about.

2

By late afternoon, introductions had been made, and Winnie and Benjamin set up a video call.

Despite his stress and his obvious lack of sleep, Dr. Benjamin Rook appeared to be a handsome man, in a rugged, outdoorsy way. Winnie knew from her research that he was fifty-four, and that he lived and worked at 11,200 feet in the mountains of Colorado, outside a small town called Worster Bend.

He wore a wool cap over his shaggy brown and gray hair. His beard, a mix of those same colors, looked nicely groomed, maybe for the conference in Frankfurt.

Winnie's skill at seeing auras never translated very well through a computer screen. But she knew kindness and decency when she saw it, and Benjamin Rook's face looked kind and decent. His troubled brown eyes gazed into the screen with such agony as he retold his story, Winnie could feel the same pain as though she'd experienced it herself.

"Do you have any idea when it happened?" she asked. She could see some of the destruction behind him. It looked like a tornado had ripped through his cabin.

"I-I think so." Benjamin held up to his camera a stack of what looked like graph paper, with long jagged lines marked across the top page.

He rubbed his fingers over his eyes and once again looked wearily at the screen.

"Has Amanda told you about my instruments?" he asked.

"No," Winnie said, picturing Benjamin playing a bassoon. She knew it must be just her active imagination, not a vision or clairvoyance. She coughed and turned her head so he wouldn't see her momentary look of surprise.

"I've built instruments, very sensitive measuring devices, to capture my plants' movements. And their..." Benjamin hesitated and let out a sigh.

"Their thoughts," Winnie supplied.

Benjamin nodded. "Amanda told you."

"No, but I felt you think it, then suppress it."

Now it was Benjamin's turn to look surprised. He

chuckled self-consciously. "I guess that's why I'm hiring you, right? You know things."

"This will work better," Winnie said, "if you share with me everything about your work. Don't worry, I won't ridicule you or judge it. I'm on your side, Benjamin."

He nodded. The poor man looked exhausted.

"And more than that," Winnie said, "from what I've read about you, I think your research sounds remarkable. I want to know more, just for myself. So go ahead. Talk my ear off." She smiled encouragingly. Benjamin seemed to perk up.

"I'm so used to people..." Benjamin took his wool cap off, vigorously scratched his hair, then pulled the cap back on and sat up straight, as though he first needed to complete that ceremony. "And especially after what's happened. I'm used to having to defend my research. To just about everyone. But if you really are a friendly ear..."

"I am. Trust me."

Winnie could see his eyes brighten. Some enthusiasm was returning to the man. "All right, then, I'll just tell you the truth. Unfiltered.

"The field of plant neurobiology—I just call it neurobotany now. It's easier, and it's accurate—it's all fairly new, by science standards. Openly studied for about fifteen or twenty years now—although that's not actually when it first started.

"There have been visionaries for a long time," Benjamin said. "Jagadish Chandra Bose studied it in India in the 1920s and 30s, Charles Darwin even took a pass at it before then, in the 1870s. But that's the ebb and flow of science. Someone will propose a new idea, he gets hammered for it—sorry, Dr. Parsons, but it usually was a *he*—"

"Call me Winnie," she said. "Go on."

"A few other scientists might see the sense in it, but there's such vehement opposition to it, they all have to go underground for a while. Still believing, still doing experiments in secret, some of them, and then one day the old guard starts dying off, and suddenly the new theory pops up again and a whole new generation of scientists say yeah, of course that's how it is."

Winnie nodded. That pattern was familiar to her, too. Theories in psychology came and went—and then returned again once some of the most vocal critics had retired or died.

"Albert Einstein *hated* quantum physics," Benjamin said. "He refused to accept it. It went against everything he believed about how physics and the universe work. But he was an old man by then, and even the greats move on. And after a while, quantum physics became the new popular kid on the block. Everyone accepts it now."

Winnie had a feeling. A sense of where Benjamin was going with this. But she let him tell it in his own way.

"Over time," he said, "some of my colleagues from around the world have been pursuing neurobotany and making a few small inroads. We get invited to the international conferences now, even though sometimes it seems like it's just for target practice. We're the targets."

"Frankfurt," Winnie said.

"And how," Benjamin said. "But ... I knew I was pushing it. Pushing *them*. But there will never be progress in this field if we don't speak up."

"What was your paper about?" Winnie asked. "The one they booed when you read it?"

"Empathy. My paper was called *Do Plants Empathize with Humans?* I couldn't believe the organizers invited me. Some of my friends tried to talk me out of going. But I can be stubborn. As you see, I paid the price. My plants did."

"Tell me what you've discovered," Winnie said.

She admired the brave. Benjamin Rook was brave. For so long, in her own life, Winnie had not been. She couldn't imagine speaking at one of the psychology conferences while she was a professor and revealing her own secret talents. Someone courageous like Benjamin might have gone public as soon as he had tenure.

But Winnie didn't want to hear it: the laughter, the ridicule, the scorn.

And she knew, human nature being what it was, that some people would hate her and try to hurt her because of her psychic abilities. That kept her afraid for a long time.

Her husband Joe had helped her climb out of that dark and frightening hole. He admired her gifts from the beginning, and relied on them without question.

Winnie was not afraid any longer. She hadn't been for a long time. She was still cautious, but that was different.

"There were a few scientists back in the 1970s," Benjamin said, "who saw little hints that their plants might actually care what happened to the people around them.

"They hooked the plants up to variations of a polygraph machine—"

"Lie detector."

"Right," Benjamin said. "And they tested the reactions of the plants to certain stimuli: fire, cutting, but also pleasant things like watering them and playing classical music."

"I remember that," Winnie said. "People thought it

was funny, but a lot of us started talking to our plants then."

"Exactly," Benjamin said. "But there were other experiments. In one lab, they noticed from the readouts that the plants reacted strongly whenever someone cut their finger, say, or when they poured brine shrimp down the drain after whatever experiments they'd been doing with them. The plants had an empathetic response. They didn't like another creature's pain or death."

"I never heard of that," said Winnie.

"No," Benjamin agreed. "A lot of this was hidden away. The scientists learned pretty quickly how unpopular their findings were. Especially among their more traditional, close-minded colleagues."

"But you continued that research," Winnie said.

"I did. It's always fascinated me, ever since I read about it when I was a kid. And you know what? Those scientists were right. I've been conducting experiments for the past fifteen years, and I've duplicated a lot of their early findings. And made a whole bunch of new ones of my own."

"Explain it to me," Winnie said. "The empathy."

She already knew in her heart that what Benjamin was saying was true. Winnie felt an affinity with the green growing inhabitants of this world. She always had, since she was a little girl. She used to sit in her back yard for hours, leaning against the giant desert oak tree there, feeling its movements deep within its cells, like blood flowing in her own veins. But she knew the life within the tree was made of water and sunlight and air. When a breeze blew through its leaves, Winnie could hear it laugh.

Of course she never told her parents. By then, she knew better. But she did scold Steven once for breaking off a branch to use as a sword when he played with one of his friends.

"That *hurts* him!" Winnie said. Steven pretended in front of his friend that Winnie was being ridiculous, but later, in private, Steven apologized. He knew his little sister could see and hear and feel things he never could. He didn't understand it, but he knew her power was real.

So Winnie did not scoff at Benjamin Rook's confession. She could see on his kind and honest face that he was telling the truth.

"My plants know me," Benjamin said. "They're ... connected to me. The same way trees in a forest share root systems and communicate through the various fungal networks. My plants have taken me into their communities. I don't know how yet—that's something I'm experimenting with right now—but somehow they seem to know what I'm *feeling*. Let me give you an example."

Benjamin paged through the sheets of paper stacked on the desk in front of him. He pulled one out and held it up to the screen.

"This is from the third day of my trip to Frankfurt. I have the readouts time stamped in two-minute increments.

"I've started keeping a very detailed journal every day. I try to record everything: what time I get up, how I feel, what I'm doing every half hour that I'm awake.

"I especially note anything that causes me any kind of emotion, whether it's worry, happiness, anger, anything other than just a baseline calm.

"Every night," Benjamin said, "I compare my journal with the readouts from the plants. And..." He looked at Winnie through the screen. "This is why people were booing me at the conference. But I have the data. I've been recording it for two years. It's solid. I can prove it."

"The plants know," Winnie said.

Benjamin nodded. "They know. Not all of them, but a large segment. Certain species are more attuned than others. My tulips have never cared about me at all." He smiled then, the first smile Winnie had seen from him yet. "But there's no question what the data shows. My plants know when I'm upset."

He held up the sheet of paper again. The lines on it spiked all across the page.

"I wasn't paying attention as I walked through Frankfurt that day," Benjamin said. "This first spike was when I stepped off the curb and almost got hit by a car. The time stamp matches it exactly. The spikes after it, and on the next several pages, are because my heart was racing for at least five minutes afterward. My plants knew something had happened to me. And they reacted in sympathy. They felt stress, too."

"Did they react when the intruder came in?" Winnie asked. If Benjamin's instruments could measure the plants' stress, this might be a way of pinpointing when the destruction happened.

"Yes. Absolutely." Benjamin thumbed through the pages at the bottom of the stack, and held up several pages for Winnie to see. "I can forward these to you—"

"Yes," Winnie said, "do. All of them from that day."

"But you can see," Benjamin said, pointing to the wild, erratic spikes on just one of the papers. "They ... it must have been horrible." His shoulders slumped and he let the paper sink to his desk. "They were ... I don't know how else to put it. They were screaming right up until they died."

Winnie saw a flash of it. A gloved hand grabbing a brown pot from among many others lined up next to it on a shelf. A winter glove, black knit with white knit on the fingertips, not a sterile Nitrile glove like someone might use in a laboratory.

The person appeared to be left-handed. He or she

held the pot in the right hand, and used the left to rip it out by the roots.

Then both hands stripped the plant's leaves and broke the stem in half. The intruder then threw the pot to the floor. Winnie could hear the clay exterior crack. She could picture a heavy winter boot wading through heaps of potting soil on the floor. She saw the lower part of a pant leg. It was black, and looked like a thick insulated ski pant.

"You said you didn't find any tracks outside your house."

"No," Benjamin said. "This time of year, it snows about every day. Based on the plant readouts, I know it happened four days ago. Too much snow since then."

"You were gone for ten days," Winnie remembered. "So this was on day six. What time?"

"It started a little after two o'clock in the afternoon."

"And what were you doing in Germany at the same time?" Winnie asked.

"Just getting home from dinner with some of my colleagues," said Benjamin. "There's an eight-hour time difference. It would have been just after ten there."

"And did you ... sense anything?" Winnie asked.

Benjamin shook his head. He seemed embarrassed, as well as sad. "The connection only seems to go one way. They know about me. I don't know about them."

Winnie considered for a moment. She still had the

images in her mind: the gloved hands, the destruction of the plant, the heavy boot and the ski pant.

"You might think this a strange question," she said, "but did the intruder urinate or defecate on anything?"

Benjamin ran a hand over his face. "Jeez. You're telling me it could have been even worse?"

Winnie didn't say so, but she was asking for a particular reason.

"No," Benjamin said. "At least not that. Just blocking up the toilet with rags, but there was nothing in it. And no … smell. In my house or the lab."

Winnie nodded. "You have enemies, of course."

"Many," said Benjamin. "I mean, not like pull-a-gun-on-me enemies, but a lot of people hate what I'm doing."

"Why?" Winnie asked. "Can you explain the anger? You're just pursuing a theory. You're not doing anyone any harm."

"Yeah, but it's like Darwin and evolution," Benjamin said. "He took something sacred—the primacy of Man—and told everyone we weren't made from clay after all, like it says in Genesis. We weren't born already masters of all we surveyed. We evolved from lesser creatures.

"I've taken something sacred, too—the notion that animals and man are the only thinking, feeling entities—and now I've dared to say that plants are on the same level. Different mechanisms, obviously—plants don't have brains—but equivalent. Some people get very, very exercised about that."

"Enough to break into your home and destroy your work."

"Yes," Benjamin said.

"You don't believe this was some random act of vandalism."

"Hell no," Benjamin answered.

"I'll need a list," Winnie said. "Of everyone you can think of who might hate you for the research you're doing. Not just jealous colleagues or skeptical friends or acquaintances. You know what hate feels like. Spend some time really seeing people in your mind's eye, and try to remember everyone who hates you or hates your work."

It felt strange to say the word *hate* out loud, and to say it so many times. It wasn't a word often used anymore in polite psychology circles.

Other words were offered in its place: distrustful, angry, *triggered*—that was the current catch-all term— but Winnie knew that the destruction of Benjamin's home and lab was an act of hatred and she would not call it something else.

"I'm ... not really sure how this works," Benjamin said. "How *you* work. Can you see it? Do you know who did it? I mean, can you describe the person to me, and I'll tell you who that is?"

"I've seen a few fragments," Winnie said, "just during our conversation. But clairvoyance has its limits—at least mine does. I don't see everything in the world all the time. I think if anyone did, it would drive them mad. I need something that helps focus my attention. I wouldn't have known anything about your situation if Amanda didn't send you to me."

Benjamin nodded. "All right, I understand that. So if I get you a list..."

"I can go through the names," Winnie said, "and see if any images come to mind. The more names you can give me, the more chances I have of finding the person who did this. So don't hold back." She smiled. "Tell me honestly about all the people who hate your guts."

Then Winnie had another thought. "You said all the plants were killed—but were they really? All of them?"

"I haven't had the heart to go back in there," Benjamin said. "But ... I suppose some of them might be horribly damaged, but still alive."

"Excellent," Winnie said. "I want you to gather any survivors for me and send them to me as quickly as you can."

She gave Benjamin her address.

"I'll take care of them," Winnie promised. "Send them in a way to keep them moist and protected. Will you do that?"

"All right."

Winnie could see that the idea that some of his plants might have survived had brought color back to Benjamin's cheeks. He had been in shock before. Winnie didn't blame him. But now she needed him to buck up and go survey the scene of the crime, and find out if it was as bad as he thought.

If she could see the plants for herself, even if it were just one or two of them...

She wasn't sure—she had never done anything like it before—but maybe she could find more answers there.

"I should go do that now," Benjamin said. "If any of them are still alive I need to get them into water."

"Ah!" Winnie said, the flash now coming clearly into her mind. "You really did play the bassoon! In high school."

Benjamin's cheeks flushed an even brighter shade of red. "All right, I'm convinced. *Nobody* knows that."

3

It wasn't easy for Ben to get his plants into Dr. Parsons's hands. (He couldn't call her Winnie, even in his head. And to her face, during their video call, Ben found it easier to call her nothing. Dr. Parsons reminded him of his stately grandmother, and the woman always had a sharp word for any young people who dared call her by her first name.)

There was the careful packing, trying to preserve what few plants had survived. Then the round-trip cross-country ski trek from his cabin to the tiny general store in Worster Bend.

"Another storm this afternoon," said Jason, the owner of the store. Ben could see Jason's wife down at the end of a nearby aisle unpacking a box and stacking cans on the shelf. "Can't guarantee this will go out today," Jason said of Ben's package. "Might not be till tomorrow, or even Friday."

Ben took the chance. As attached as he was to his plants, he had done what he could for now. He left them at the store and skied home.

Where he spent the next two days cleaning and clearing, trying to ignore the desperate pain in his heart. This was his life, and his life's work.

He wasn't old yet, but he wasn't young, either. It wouldn't take him fifteen years to return to whole, but it might take five or six or eight.

He had known for years that he should pause, stop driving forward every day, and instead make duplicates of his instruments, the ones he had proven to himself would work.

But every day brought new discoveries, and Ben could never make himself stop. All of his delicate, precision instruments were completely unique. He would have to assemble the materials again and try to build them from scratch. And he might not get it right again. He was generally optimistic by nature, but he was also a realist. All of the equipment the intruder had smashed onto his floor might never exist again. And that had been Ben's own fault.

There were other faults, too. It was easy to catalog them during the sad, monotonous hours of sweeping up glass and pottery and dirt.

He should have been more diplomatic with his elders. Less combative and, he had to admit to himself, not so cocky. He understood why he did it—the constant nay-saying by more senior members of the scientific community wore a person down. Sometimes the only way Ben could face it was to pretend to be more confident than he actually was.

But as he reviewed fifteen years of interactions with his colleagues, maybe it wasn't such a surprise that so many of them hated him.

Ben was still working on a list of enemies to give Dr. Parsons. The first twenty-six names had come to him quickly, easily.

He wondered idly if it was this way for everyone. If he asked the owner of the general store in Worster Bend if he could name twenty-six enemies off the top of his head, how long would it take the man?

After the first spate of names, Ben had set the list aside for a whole day. He didn't feel good about it. It was like some pearly-gates life review that made him re-examine his many errors.

But he had hired Dr. Parsons to help him, and they wouldn't get any closer to a solution until Ben stopped moping around.

He opened the file on his computer again—simply labeled Enemies—and mentally replayed the past several years of interactions, searching his memory for more names.

He shouldn't limit it to professional relationships. He had had a few disappointing personal relationships, too. But were those old lovers enemies now? As far as Ben knew, they had all parted not exactly as friends, but not with hatred, either.

It was hard to make a life with a man living in a little cabin in the woods who spent nearly every waking hour interacting with his plants.

But Ben hadn't been willing to give it up for any of them, and to be fair, none of them had asked him to. It was simply one of the sacrifices scientists—or anyone with a passion for their work—made to pursue their chosen obsession.

Ben did an internet search of the various conferences he had attended over the past few years, hoping to refresh his memory about all of the other presenters who had been there.

He added seven more names to his list. Did those people truly hate him, or only want him to fail? Sometimes it was hard to know the difference.

"Well, this is cheerful," Ben said out loud to his wounded cabin.

If any of the plants in the nearby lab heard him, if any of them empathized with him, he couldn't know. Not without his instruments.

And the only living plants in the lab right now were the roots of a tomato plant and a tulip—an unfriendly tulip—that Ben had managed to salvage from the piles of plant parts on the floor.

He had kept these two back, as a sort of token to himself. He could rebuild ... if he decided to. He could start again with just these two plants.

The other four survivors he had sent to Dr. Parsons. A bright red rose hip that had escaped being smushed; the hardy leaf of a nearly indestructible philodendron that Ben routinely pruned every year, starting new plants from the cuttings; a single stem of a white geranium that was still whole and plump, even though all the flowers had been ripped from it; and a short segment of a climbing bean stalk, robbed of its beans but still alive.

Ben had built them a special cocoon for transport. He hoped they would reach Dr. Parsons still intact.

In the meantime, in between sweeping and cleaning and clearing, he would continue cataloguing all the people who wished him ill.

4

———

The box arrived at Winnie's house a week after she first spoke to Benjamin Rook. The package looked slightly misshapen after its long journey, but when she opened it she could see that the wrappings around the plants were still moist.

Winnie reached for the bean stalk first. And saw a flash of a hand.

The same black knit glove she had seen before, with white on the ends of the fingers. Tearing off bean pods and ripping them in half. Then throwing them onto the floor and mashing them into the wood.

It was interesting, the person taking that many separate steps. Interesting for two reasons. First, the intruder must have felt that he or she had enough time. The person had to know that Benjamin Rook was away in Frankfurt and wouldn't return for several more days.

Second, Winnie could imagine someone else coming into the lab and giving it a wholesale demolition. Not going from plant to plant, ripping each one apart individually, but bringing in some blunt instrument like a baseball bat instead, and smashing everything in more efficient waves.

The glass and metal instruments Benjamin had made would be easily destroyed that way, too. But now came the image to Winnie's mind of the gloved hands breaking levers, snapping and bending wires, attending to the glass pieces separately by detaching them and hurling them to the floor.

Again, baseball bat. One hit. Done. But the intruder had taken minutes at a time to break apart Benjamin's many pieces of equipment one by one.

Why? Winnie didn't know. But it was a detail she tucked away to let her mind work on it while she wasn't paying attention.

She often tackled puzzles in her life this way. More often than not, the solution would come to her as she stood in the shower at night. The answer popped up in her mind like toast in a toaster.

Next Winnie removed the plump red rose hip. It was the size and shape of a blueberry. Winnie held it up to her nose to smell. It smelled earthy, woodsy, not like a rose at all. It was the fruit of the rose bush and had an identity all its own.

A flash of the boot, black, heavy, with some kind of insulation poking out the top. The boot grinding other rose hips into the floor. A fate this little one had escaped.

"What did you see?" Winnie asked the group of survivors. "Show me. I want to help."

She removed a stem from Benjamin's box. Just a stem, with a tiny white tendril of root still trailing from its base.

Winnie lifted the stem to her nose, too, but couldn't detect what it was that way.

She closed her eyes. "Show me." She gently twirled the stem between her thumb and forefinger.

She saw a white flower. A lovely cluster of soft white petals with a delicate red pistil in the center. A scent drifted into Winnie's nose, not from this stem, but from the image forming in Winnie's mind.

The scent of a geranium. "Ah. You'll be beautiful again," she told the injured plant. "I promise." She set it on top of the wet towel she had laid on her kitchen counter, and reached for the fourth and last survivor.

At the first touch, the philodendron flooded Winnie's mind with pictures.

The woman's long brown hair, hanging in a long

braid down her back. A red fleece hat pulled down low over her ears.

Not the woman's face, Winnie couldn't see that from where the philodendron must have watched, but she saw the woman's back all the way down to her boots. She wore a bright blue insulated ski jacket over black insulated pants.

Winnie had already suspected it would be a woman, after learning that the intruder hadn't urinated or defecated in any of the rooms or on top of the debris.

She had read a study years ago by a psychologist who analyzed various criminal behaviors in both men and women.

Men liked to mark. They saw it as a kind of domination, a way to further humiliate their victims by despoiling their possessions. And, according to the psychologist's research, men had fewer inhibitions against urinating and even defecating in public.

Whereas women felt vulnerable exposing themselves that way. Women committed other kinds of despoiling, the psychologist said, such as shredding and ripping their victim's clothing, smashing breakable items, and even tearing apart containers of food to spill the contents everywhere, making for a smelly, time-consuming clean up.

It was foolish to generalize, Winnie knew, but the information was interesting nonetheless. She knew that the psychologist was not claiming that men *always*, or women *never*.

But she often read a colleague's research and tested it against her own experience. She found that particular study compelling. She thought that several of his conclusions were probably right.

The kind of destruction at Benjamin's house and lab fit with that research profile. The way the intruder took the time to rip and break and smash. The blocking of the toilet. The propping open of the freezer.

The intruder wanted Benjamin to come home not only to destruction, but also to a *mess*. Something that would take more than a few days to clear away. Something that would make Benjamin despair, that might make him wish he could just burn the cabin and his lab and walk away and never return.

Winnie closed her eyes and tried to feel it. Tried to feel the emotions radiating from the woman. Tried to feel her through the fragment of a philodendron who had witnessed what happened that day.

What was the woman's motive? Not just hatred— that was too general a term. Winnie needed to be more specific.

What did the woman *want*? That was the right question. What did she hope would happen when Benjamin Rook opened the door and saw what she did?

Give up. Leave. Go.

She wanted Benjamin to quit.

She wanted to take the fight out of him. She wanted him to see it was impossible to begin again.

Winnie continued pressing the philodendron leaf between her fingers, letting the plant connect her to the past. Winnie watched from the philodendron's vantage, but she could also feel herself there inside that room, an invisible presence observing on her own.

Winnie could see the woman from the back, her long brown braid dancing against her spine as she ripped apart plants and hurled them to the floor and grinded them under her boot.

The woman turned slightly to the left, to grab the next plant in line.

Winnie could see the woman's grim smile. As though this were a long, grueling job she had to do, but the woman found satisfaction in doing it well.

The woman picked up one of the instruments set between two of the plants and she actually let out a shriek as she began breaking it apart.

A most unpleasant sound. It was the first sound Winnie had heard her make.

The laboratory was warm with the respiration of vegetation and with whatever heating Benjamin had set up for the room.

Although the woman might have felt comfortable inside the cabin, where the temperature might have been lower, here in the lab Winnie could see that the woman's efforts were making her sweat.

She paused in her destruction long enough to unzip her blue ski coat and take it off.

Winnie looked eagerly for some kind of identifying writing on the shirt underneath. An insignia from some college or organization. Something to give her a clue.

But even though the woman wore a plain black sweater underneath her coat, there was a clue there after all.

Winnie let go of the philodendron. She had seen enough.

She hurried to her computer and summoned Benjamin Rook to a video call.

5

____

Winnie described the woman she saw. "Mid-thirties, long brown hair in a braid, fit-looking, and pregnant."

For a moment, Benjamin looked confused.

Then a light seemed to dawn in his eyes.

"No."

"You know her," Winnie said.

Benjamin nodded slowly, a little dazedly, as though waking from a dream.

"Marsha Haggerty," he said.

Marsha. Was that why Winnie had thought of that childhood memory, of Marsha betraying her to their pastor when they were ten? The memory had popped into Winnie's mind during her first video call with Benjamin.

Had popped into her mind like toast out of a toaster.

Even after sixty-eight years of living with her clairvoyant mind, Winnie was still learning exactly how it worked. Here was another lesson. She needed to pay closer attention to her thoughts, even when they seemed to be unconnected and random.

"Who is she?" Winnie asked. "One of your colleagues?"

"No. She and her husband Jason own the general store up the road. And they're my neighbors. About a quarter mile away."

"She's pregnant?"

Benjamin nodded.

"Why would she do it?" Winnie asked.

"Because they want my land," Benjamin said. "Marsha's father is a developer. He came to me last fall with a big offer, but I didn't even think about it. I told him no."

"What kind of offer?"

"Over a million. But it's chicken change to him. He'd make it all back before long. There's a ski resort not far from here. Last summer they announced they're expanding over to one of the mountains on our side. Marsha's father has a whole plan for building vacation homes up here. I told him good luck, but I'm not selling. I've worked too hard getting my lab just the way I want. I told him I can never move."

"How did he react?"

"He seemed pretty professional about it," said Benjamin. "Told me if I change my mind, call him. And Jason at the store never treated me any differently."

"What about Marsha?"

"Friendly smile, but we don't really talk."

"Were any of them on your enemies list?" Winnie asked.

"No. None of them. I thought everything was fine."

Winnie and Benjamin both sat at their respective computers, not saying anything, only thinking.

Finally Winnie spoke. "What will you do?"

Benjamin ran a hand over his face. He looked tired again. Winnie couldn't blame him. It was a lot to take in. A lot to consider.

"I don't have any real proof," Benjamin said. "Just you. No security cameras, nothing I could show the sheriff."

"No fingerprints," Winnie said. "She wore gloves."

"And she's pregnant," Benjamin said. "Am I really going to get her arrested?"

"She destroyed your home and your life's work," Winnie said.

Benjamin sighed and shook his head.

"I've lived here for fifteen years. They bought the place next to me about three years ago. Bought the store, too. So what am I supposed to do? Avoid them? Pretend this never happened? I'd see them whenever I went in to the store."

"And you'd know what Marsha did," Winnie said.

"I'd know. And I'd know she got away with it."

"So what do you want to do?" Winnie asked again. "Stay or go? Sell to her father and start over someplace else?"

"No," Benjamin said firmly. "I want to stay. Truth is, I love it here. But I'll have to start over from scratch. It's going to take me years to get back on my feet."

"And money," Winnie said.

"A lot of money," Benjamin agreed.

Winnie saw a flash of an image, one she had seen before. She was back in Benjamin's lab. She could smell the earthy scent of the plants and feel the warmth of the heated room.

Marsha Haggerty let out her strange shriek as she destroyed one of Benjamin's instruments.

Winnie could see the woman sweating. Marsha unzipped her ski coat and took it off.

But not before a drop of sweat slid down Marsha's face.

The image seemed magnified. As though Winnie had the ability to zoom in. And that magnification continued as the drop of sweat fell through the air. Winnie could hear the soft *plink* it made on the metal surface of the broken instrument lying on the wooden floor.

Then the flash ended. Winnie knew her mind must have shown her that for a reason.

"Where is all the debris from your lab?" she asked Benjamin. "Do you still have it?"

He nodded. "It's too much for me to haul out on my skis. I'll have to wait for spring to load it in a trailer and drive it to the dump."

Winnie smiled. "Good. Hang onto it." Maybe they could do something after all.

Winnie was not by nature a liar. Sometimes she pretended to be someone else for the sake of her clients' cases, but that was deception for a good cause.

The few times she had tried an outright lie, Winnie could feel a dark fog creeping into her mind. Her clairvoyance was a gift. She never wanted to do anything to interfere with it.

So she could not lie to Marsha Haggerty, and she couldn't ask Benjamin to do it, either. If justice was going to be done, Winnie needed her consciousness to be clean.

"Will you write me a special science paper?" she asked Benjamin. "I'll tell you what needs to be in it. The sooner the better. The Haggertys have probably watched crime dramas on TV. They might have an idea how this all works."

6

A *Drop of Sweat: Using DNA from the Crime Scene to Find the Pregnant Woman Who Destroyed my Laboratory*, by Dr. Benjamin Rook.

Winnie thought it was a page-turner.

So did Jason Haggerty, who read it on the counter at his store. It had come in over the rarely-used fax machine that he kept for customers who didn't have email or a scanner.

The fax was addressed to Benjamin Rook. The cover letter was from someone called Dr. Amanda Birkauer from the University of Arizona. *Looks great! Hope they catch her! Keep me posted!*

"Marsha?" Jason called into the stock room. "MARSHA!"

Scientific papers could be very dry. Not intended for the public.

But Winnie had made a few suggestions to help Benjamin write a paper that was more accessible to the average reader.

What Benjamin wrote was strictly true. He didn't reveal his source. He didn't say that a clairvoyant had seen a pregnant brunette destroy the lab, and had watched her DNA-rich sweat fall onto a metal surface.

Benjamin didn't say that the broken fragments of some of his plants had provided the link for that clairvoyant to see who had committed the crime.

He did use the kind of TV language that people have come to know: swab, DNA sequencing, bingo. And the paper included a photograph of one of the delicate, broken instruments, leaving it for the reader to assume that the perpetrator's sweat had been collected from it and then analyzed by experts.

A short time later, without asking, without doing anything but placing an order at the general store for twenty new terra cotta pots and some potting soil and seeds, Benjamin Rook received an offer.

But this time, not an offer for his land.

Jason Haggerty pushed a sealed letter across the counter to Ben. "Been waiting for you to come in," Jason said. "Letter came for you last week." The owner of the general store bit a hangnail on his thumb. He seemed a little nervous. Ben pretended not to notice.

Ben opened the letter right there. He had no secrets from Jason Haggerty.

The letter was from Jason's father-in-law. The developer who was about to become a grandfather for the first time.

The terms were fair. The surprise donation to support Dr. Benjamin Rook's research was generous.

"It's a start," Ben said, smiling at Jason. Then Ben upped his order for pots and potting soil and seeds. It looked like he was back in business.

He scanned a copy of the letter and emailed it to Dr. Parsons.

"Satisfied?" Winnie asked him.

"I wish none of it had ever happened," Ben said, "but yes. Considering everything, I'm satisfied."

He would have sufficient funding to rebuild, and funding beyond that to continue his work for the next several years.

And he didn't have to wrestle with the idea of seeing his pregnant neighbor arrested.

Winnie clicked off their video call and returned to the kitchen. She'd been baking peanut butter cookies. The smell of them lifted her soul.

On the window sill above her sink, in small pretty pots, grew four young plants Winnie was currently nurturing. When they were strong enough, she would plant them with others of their kind inside and outside the house: with her flowers, her vegetables, and the philodendron that had already taken over Winnie's office and was climbing all over her shelves.

"He says hi," Winnie told the young plants. Even though Benjamin hadn't. But it wasn't strictly a lie. He would have said it if he remembered the plants were here.

Because Dr. Benjamin Rook knew what Winnie knew now, too.

The plants were always listening.

THE LONG GRAY HOOK

The February morning air was cold, but the winter sun felt golden and warm on Winnie's face. This was the best time of year in Tucson: chilly days, but always a blue sky. It lifted the spirit the way a cloudy, gloomy day never could. There was a reason people chose to live in the desert, despite the broiling heat of summer.

Winnie dug her gloved hands into the pockets of her purple fleece vest and watched her yellow Labrador cavort on the long stretch of university grass. She had named the dog Clover because of a childhood book Winnie read so many times the edges of the cardboard cover were worn away as if mice had gnawed them.

Winnie's mother had never allowed any pets. She

kept a clean house, and a dog or cat would make everything feel hairy and dirty.

Winnie's brother, Steven, got away with a gerbil temporarily, until his mother heard scratching inside Steven's dresser and found the little nest he had made for the animal there.

A shriek, some tears, and the gerbil was gone to a neighborhood friend's house within the hour.

Winnie had pled her case as many times as she dared, but her mother never budged.

Winnie had promised herself she would have as many cats and dogs as she wanted once she moved out and lived on her own. But then her life became hectic. College, grad school, pursuing her PhD, then becoming a professor, a wife...

And finally one day, her husband told Winnie to close her eyes, and she could hear the front door open and close.

Before Joe was two steps out the door, Winnie saw it inside her mind. A flash of a yellow ball of fur. The open, panting mouth, the pink tongue between white puppy teeth.

There was no point in pretending. Joe knew all about Winnie's gifts. She sprang to her feet and hurried out after him and held her arms open wide to gather in her very own dog. Finally. Clover.

That was a little over seven years ago. Clover had been Winnie's birthday present.

And now today, February third, was Joe's birthday. He would have been seventy-two years old if he were still alive.

Winnie had toasted him this morning with her first mug of coffee. She still loved him. She always would.

And it added an extra layer of affection for the yellow Lab currently playing on the University of Arizona lawn. Winnie watched Clover roll in the crisp grass, melting the thin layer of sparkling frost with her thick and tawny winter coat.

Winnie smiled to think of the man who had brought a puppy home thinking he might actually surprise his clairvoyant wife for once.

Winnie saw movement in the distance. A woman jogging toward them, her right arm raised in a wave.

Dr. Amanda Birkauer was in her early fifties, but she moved like any of the young college students Winnie saw out on this same campus jogging in the early mornings.

Amanda wore her long brown hair in a ponytail, threaded through a navy blue University of Arizona ball cap, and wore her usual uniform of dark blue athletic pants and matching jacket, both branded with the U of A logo. She looked like a coach, rather than a professor.

She was Winnie's former colleague in the Psychology department, and one of her best friends.

Amanda was also Assistant Director of the university's mind lab—also known as the parapsychology research lab. Winnie had been one of the lab's test subjects for years.

"Just the person," Amanda said as she jogged the remaining few yards. Her cheeks looked flushed from exercising in the winter cold.

Clover ran to meet her and stood wagging her tail, waiting for Amanda's customary greeting. Amanda knelt in front of the dog and fluffed up her fur at the shoulders, kissed Clover on the forehead, and hugged her around her neck.

The dog wagged so hard she could have achieved liftoff.

Amanda gave Winnie a quick hug, too. Then she stood with her hands on her hips and got down to business.

"I have a medical mystery for you."

Winnie scoffed. "You know that isn't my strength." She had some skill with medical intuition, but not reliably, and not on command.

She might catch a glimpse of someone's insides, like seeing an X-Ray from the corner of her eye, but the image could disappear as quickly as it came. Winnie was still trying to improve her ability there.

"You always say that," Amanda said, "but you're still better than a lot of others I've seen. Besides, it's your credentials she wants. You're respectable."

Winnie raised her eyebrows. "All right, tell me."

Amanda threaded her arm through Winnie's and walked with her along the grassy mall. Clover returned to her own occupation of rolling in the frost.

"Do you know Lila Merchant in the Dance department?"

"I know of her," Winnie said. "We've never met."

Dr. Lila Merchant had made a splash in New York as a ballerina in her younger years, then retired before the company dropped her once her age and injuries made her less of an attraction.

She enrolled in college and eventually earned her PhD. She had been a professor for the past twenty years or so. She was around Winnie's age, in her late sixties.

"She must be close to retirement," Winnie said.

"I don't think so," Amanda said. "Check with her when she's ninety."

Clover came bounding over for another dose of attention. Amanda obliged, flipping Clover's ears back and forth. The dog happily panted, then ran away again.

"It's good I'm not jealous," Winnie said, smiling. "I love that she loves you."

The clock at the Student Union in the center of campus clanged out the hour. Amanda checked her watch. "I have to run in a minute. I'll tell you fast. Several of the kids in the Dance department have been coming down with some strange symptoms lately. Nausea, fainting, weakness. Lila has done everything she can think of. Sent them to doctors, blood tests, the works. Nothing. Then she had the building checked—vents, mold, switched food services—she'll tell you all about it.

"But the worst was last week," Amanda continued. "One of the girls did one of those jumps—I don't know what it's called, that one where they do the splits in the air and they look like gazelles—"

"I don't know, either," Winnie said, "but I know what you mean."

The words flashed in her mind.

"Oh," she blurted out. "Grand *jeté*."

Amanda laughed. She was used to Winnie's unexpected knowledge. "Yes, that one. Lila said the girl had done it since she was a child, no problem, but this time she came crashing down and broke her leg."

"That's terrible!"

"The girl didn't know what happened," Amanda said. "She said she just lost all her strength. So Lila has had it now. She's desperate. No one can find out what's wrong." Amanda checked her watch again. "Gotta go. Thirty seconds. Short story, I told her what you can do.

She remembers you from faculty. She wants to hire you right away. She thinks no one will object because you used to be a psychology professor."

Amanda began jogging backward away from Winnie. "So, will you do it?"

"It's not my best thing," Winnie said. "Can't you recommend someone else?"

"Another psychic who used to be a psychology professor?" Amanda said, picking up her backward pace. "I'm all out of those. Come on, Win. Just talk to her. For me. See if you get any kind of feeling. She's really stressed."

"Send me her number," Winnie said. Even if she couldn't help Lila Merchant, she could at least be a sympathetic ear. Winnie might be able to think of an experienced medical intuitive who could help her. She didn't want to say a flat no.

Amanda blew Winnie a kiss, then turned and took off at sprint toward the Psychology building. Clover wagged her tail as she watched Amanda fly.

"I know," Winnie told her. "You wish I could run like that."

Amanda Birkauer competed in triathlons. Clover would have to settle for Winnie's pace.

Winnie turned toward her right. From where she stood, she could see in the distance the dramatic architecture of the Dance department building. She had never been inside it. There were many buildings on campus she only knew from the outside.

Unlike the standard brick construction of so many of the buildings, the Dance department lived in a nest of steel and glass as artistic as what must go on inside. Winnie was happy for an excuse to look inside it at last —if she decided to take Lila Merchant's case.

But even if Winnie referred her on to someone else, she could still satisfy her curiosity. Set up a meeting with Lila in person.

"Come on, Clove," Winnie called to the grass-covered dog. She held out the leash and the Labrador trotted to Winnie's side. It was a trick Winnie never taught the dog. Clover had decided on her own that she wanted to do it.

Winnie strode back across campus in the sparkling morning light. On this cold winter morning she felt a fresh spring in her step.

Winnie couldn't help smiling to herself. Amanda Birkauer knew her too well. She had strummed Winnie's strings. Winnie could feel the vibration in her mind, could feel the questions already assembling.

Weakness. Nausea. Fainting. And now a girl with a broken leg. Why? And why hadn't any of the medical tests turned up an answer?

There would be no turning away now. Winnie had to satisfy her curiosity. She would contact Professor Merchant the moment she and Clover arrived home.

And then she'd do her best to find out what was happening to those kids.

2

Winnie could hear the relief in Lila Merchant's voice over the phone. "You'll do it? You'll help us?"

Winnie hesitated. There was the matter of her fee, always. She charged lawyer prices, to make sure her clients would take her advice just as seriously. All of her years teaching Consumer Psychology had taught Winnie the value of perception.

She began to broach the subject, when Lila Merchant cut her off. "Of course," Lila said. "The Foundation will pay. We wouldn't dream of asking you to do it for free. Will you come here today? I'm free all afternoon."

That suited Winnie just fine. She was as anxious as Lila Merchant.

But the woman who met Winnie in the lobby of the Dance building a few hours later wasn't at all what Winnie expected.

The inside of the Dance building reminded Winnie of a ship. All of the furnishings, the wide banister on the stairs leading up to the second floor, and the warm, immaculate floors were made of dark polished wood, the way she imagined a luxury ocean liner might look.

She could smell the wood and the polish. It reminded her of all the woodworking Joe used to do in his spare time.

There were portraits on the walls of Lila Merchant and the other faculty, painted by someone who understood how to coax beautiful skin tones out of oils.

The artist had perfectly captured Lila Merchant's pale blue eyes, and had given her the type of tender smile a grandmother might bestow on her grandchildren.

The portrait might have been painted ten or fifteen years ago. The photograph of Professor Merchant on the Dance department website was taken more recently, maybe five years ago.

Although she couldn't say when, Winnie remembered seeing Dr. Merchant in person, at least from afar. She had stored away some memory of a bird-like woman with small bones and a graceful, elegant way of moving, as though she were still on stage.

But something was wrong with Lila Merchant. Anyone could see that, with or without Winnie's gifts.

The professor looked half her normal height. Some problem with her spine had bent Lila Merchant at the waist, so that her body now formed an upside down L, supported by the short wooden cane she used to slowly make her way across the lobby.

Her hair, which Winnie remembered seeing in a sleek gray bun on top of her head, the way ballerinas wore it for performances, now hung in thin wisps from her scalp, like the fibers on the husk of a coconut.

She looked ancient. Decades older than she really was. And she moved as if every bone in her body hurt. Winnie didn't want the professor to have to take another step. She gently guided Lila to one of the polished wooden benches in the lobby and steadied her as she sat down.

Lila sighed. Winnie could see the pain flicker across her face.

Lila lifted her head as best she could on her stiffly bent neck, and stared into Winnie's green eyes with her own pale blue ones.

"What do you see?" Lila asked.

Winnie understood the question. "Nothing. I'm sorry. I'm ... trying."

It wasn't strictly true. Winnie could see Lila Merchant's aura, the band of light surrounding Lila's body. Winnie could see that it was ripped in at least twenty different places, its tattered white edges lightly swaying as though in a breeze.

But she could not see inside Lila's body. She tried scanning it again, from Lila's wispy gray hair down to the soft black flats on her feet, but no image flashed into Winnie's mind. Her medical intuition had once again proven an unreliable tool.

But her clairvoyance was as reliable as ever. And now Winnie saw an image after all. Of Lila Merchant waking this morning, curled up in bed in her faded lavender nightgown, her body wrapped inward on itself in pain.

Winnie lightly squeezed Lila's fragile forearm. "I'm so sorry. When did this begin?"

"Last year," said Lila.

"What happened?" Although they had only just met, Winnie didn't hesitate to ask Lila such personal questions. In her experience, people wanted to be asked.

Lila lowered her gaze to her blue-veined hands gripping the top of her cane. "Unfortunately, I was in a car accident." Winnie could hear the strain in her voice.

She wondered now why Amanda hadn't told her any of this before when describing Lila Merchant's case. It must have been because Amanda was in such a hurry this morning.

Even though Winnie couldn't do anything to fix Lila

Merchant's damaged spine, she would have liked to know ahead of time about the poor woman's condition.

Whether or not Dr. Merchant sensed Winnie's question, she volunteered the answer on her own.

"I don't ... see people anymore," she said. "Just my students and my colleagues here in Dance."

"How did you contact Amanda Birkauer?" Winnie asked, although now she could guess the answer.

"I telephoned her this morning," Lila said. "I thought she might know someone who could help. Someone with ... extra abilities. You see, I've run out of ideas. And my children here, I need to protect them."

The children. The students. Winnie had gotten sidetracked. She returned her focus to the case.

"What do you think is happening?" she asked.

Lila shrugged her stooped, bony shoulders. "Poison, perhaps? Some kind of toxin the doctors can't detect? I don't know. Someone might think me paranoid..."

"But it's real," Winnie said. "What your students are feeling."

"Yes," Lila said. "It is."

A bell rang within the building. It had a gentler, more musical sound than the clock that bonged from the tower in front of the Student Union, in part because this bell had a shorter distance to travel. But the beautiful polished wood all around them seemed to deepen the notes, mellowing them like the woodwind instruments in an orchestra.

The lobby filled with students, male and female, some dressed in street clothes, some wearing leotards and tights as though they were on their way to or had just finished a dance class.

A slender young woman worked her way across the lobby floor on a pair of crutches. She wore a long-sleeved white T-shirt and navy blue running pants zipped open on the right side to accommodate the cast on her leg.

"That's her," Lila said. "Daphne? Would you come here a moment?" Lila motioned with her crooked hand.

Winnie guessed the girl was around nineteen or twenty. She had lively brown eyes and long blonde hair she wore in a ponytail high on her head. She said something to the dark-haired girl beside her who appeared to be carrying Daphne's book bag along with her own.

The friend continued at Daphne's side as the two of them made their way to Lila and Winnie.

"This is Dr. Parsons," Lila said. "I told her about your fall. She would like to know more, if you have time right now."

Winnie hadn't expected to question any of the students quite yet. In fact, she still wasn't certain she was right for this case.

And yet...

She felt great sympathy for Lila Merchant. That smiling woman in the portrait on the nearby wall appeared to be a version of Lila in some other life. The woman sitting beside Winnie now seemed broken in more ways than just her bent spine.

Even if Winnie needed to find a much more skilled medical intuitive who could consult on the case, she didn't want to let go of the case entirely. She felt involved already and wanted to help. Her heart was telling her to see this through.

Daphne maneuvered her crutches and lowered herself to a spot on the wooden bench next to Winnie. Her friend, whom Lila Merchant introduced as Carmen, set down the two book bags and patiently waited.

"What do you have now?" Lila asked them both.

"Dance History," they said together.

"You can miss the first ten minutes," Lila told them with a smile. "I'm sure someone will share their notes."

Winnie wondered why Lila didn't send Carmen on to class, but it must be because the girl was helping Daphne get around on her crutches.

"Please tell Dr. Parsons about how you were feeling before you fell."

Doctor Parsons. It was her correct title, but Winnie wondered if the girls might think she was a medical doctor instead of a PhD. In any case, she felt no need to clarify her credentials.

"I thought I was fine," Daphne said. "I've been kind of up and down this semester, but on Friday I felt pretty good."

"We had our first exhibitions," Carmen chimed in. "I was going to go after Daph. A few of us were waiting in the wings for our turn."

"I was a little nervous, but not bad," Daphne said. Her brown eyes looked earnest. The girl wasn't shy. Winnie appreciated that. Daphne had a confidence Winnie could feel.

Her aura was bright blue. It was pleasing to Winnie's eyes. She liked this girl. She could see that Daphne had a happy, positive spirit.

Her friend's aura was yellow with a band of green around her waist. The colors reminded Winnie of a sunflower.

The girls were honest. Winnie could feel that. She knew they would try to help her investigation if they could.

"And then," Daphne said, "right before I went out ... it was like this gloom settled over the whole stage. Like I was stepping out into this wet gray fog. Even though the lights were shining and my music was playing, and I should have been excited ... it just felt bad. You know? *I* felt bad."

"In what way?" Winnie asked. "Can you describe it?"

"Like..." Daphne closed her eyes for a moment, as if

trying to remember more clearly. She opened them again and looked up at Carmen.

"What did you say the other day?" Daphne asked her. "Carmen felt it, too," Daphne told Winnie. "You said it was like—"

"Like scum," Carmen said. "Like the scum around a kitchen drain. All brown and gross and slimy."

"But gray," Daphne said. "Slimy and gray for me."

Winnie tried to picture it, but she wasn't sure she understood.

Daphne lifted her hands and twisted them in the air. "Kind of gooey and messy..." Winnie pictured Daphne's hands trapped in long ropes of taffy. "But also like a fog," Daphne said. "Like something clouding my brain." She let her hands drop and she sighed. "I know none of this makes any sense. I'm sorry."

Winnie looked up at Carmen, who stood with a young dancer's grace at the end of the wooden bench. She hadn't slouched against the wall like other kids her age might do. She held her body in an erect, yet relaxed posture.

"You felt it before, too," Winnie said. "When? At the performance?"

Carmen waved her hand, like shooing a fly. "Then, before then, lots of times."

"Since when?" Winnie asked. "Can you pinpoint a date?"

Daphne and Carmen looked at each other. "I don't know," Daphne said, "maybe since last November? Some time before winter break, I know that much. Because I was starting to feel so much better those few weeks at home. Then we came back to school in mid-January, and..." Her answer trailed off. Her shoulders slouched. Winnie could feel the girl's tiredness. Maybe it was time for her to go to class.

"I think it was earlier than that for me," Carmen said. "September or October. It's hard to remember a specific time. But I was just dragging last year. And then it was just like with Daphne—I started feeling better over winter break. Then school started again. And ugh. Brown scum."

"And what are your symptoms?" Winnie asked the girls.

"Tired all the time," Daphne said. "Foggy brain, like I said."

"Bitchy," Carmen said. She laughed at Daphne's reaction. "Me, not you. Don't you think? Don't I seem a little ... I don't know, grouchy? Crabby?"

"Maybe with some people," Daphne said. "Not really with me."

Carmen rolled her eyes. "Yeah, with some people. Although I'm trying to be better."

Something in her tone made Winnie curious.

Although she wouldn't know any of the players, she wondered who they were talking about.

"Anyway," Daphne said. "It's mostly just feeling like I could take a nap any time. Then even when I do nap, I still feel so tired."

"And is that how you felt before you went out on stage last Friday?" Winnie asked. "Tired?"

"Tired and ... wrong. Like my arms and legs weren't working right. I started my jump, and I knew it the minute I left the ground. But then it was too late." She glanced down at the cast on her leg. Winnie could see the girl's sadness.

"What about you?" Winnie asked Carmen. "Did you have a problem with your performance?"

"We never got to it," Carmen said. "Everything shut down after Daphne fell."

"Oh, of course," Winnie said. She should have realized that. Yet she still sensed that Carmen could tell her more.

"But until then," Winnie said, "were you excited about your performance? Did you feel well? Or was it brown sludge?"

"Scum," Carmen corrected her, laughing. "But I think I like sludge better. I was pretty pumped when I got there, but I don't know. Maybe that was starting to go away a little. It's hard to really remember."

Winnie was silent for a moment, pondering. She

looked to her right, at Lila Merchant. "I think that's all for now," Winnie said.

Lila nodded. "Thank you, girls. Dr. Parsons might want to talk to you again later. You've both been very helpful."

Daphne set her crutches underneath her armpits and pushed off from the bench. Carmen helped steady her as she stood. Then Carmen retrieved their book bags from the floor.

Winnie liked to see little kindnesses like that, a friend helping her friend. The gesture was so natural, Winnie could see that it was in Carmen's character to be kind.

It made her wonder again about what Carmen said, about being grouchy, but trying to do better.

Tired, grouchy, foggy-headed. They were the kind of symptoms people experienced when they tried to give up caffeine. But they could also be caused by other dietary changes, like being too dehydrated or having low blood sugar.

"Do you girls eat?" Winnie asked. "I can imagine a dance program might make you want to—"

"Oh, I eat," Carmen said, laughing. "I won't even tell you what." She glanced at Professor Merchant with a hint of guilt.

"The students are required to take nutrition class-es," Lila Merchant said. She pointed at Carmen with an indulgent smile. "Greens, grains, beans for protein..."

"At least one piece of fruit every day," Carmen said. "That one I do for sure."

"We eat," Daphne assured Winnie. "And over winter break, I *really* ate. We're working out so much all the time, if we didn't, we'd pass out." She looked at the cast on her leg and frowned. "Even more than lately."

Again, Winnie could feel the girls' honesty. She would have to dig deeper to find an answer.

"I'll let you go," she told the two girls. "Thank you for telling me all of this. If you think of anything else you want to tell me, please email me." She gave Daphne and Carmen her address. Both girls typed it into their phones.

Winnie watched the two of them make their slow way across the lobby toward their classroom. Carmen carried both of their book bags strung across opposite shoulders. Yet even with that burden, the girl still carried herself as though she were gliding.

Even in her younger years, Winnie had never had grace like that, she was sure of it.

"Any thoughts?" Lila asked.

"Nothing concrete," Winnie said. "But I was interested in how the girls described it. I'd like to talk to more of the students. How many would you say are having these kinds of symptoms?"

Lila considered. "There might be about twenty of them in all, but I'd say seven or eight of them have it the worst."

"Then can you set up interviews?" Winnie asked. "Starting tomorrow. I want to go think before I talk to any more of them."

But she didn't just want to think. Winnie needed to do research. As much as she relied on her clairvoyance and intuition, she also depended on grounding herself in facts.

Home again that evening, while Clover chewed an antler on the couch, Winnie searched on her computer for information about the accident that had crippled Lila Merchant.

And found that Lila had omitted a substantial part of the truth.

3

The accident had not been Lila Merchant's fault, nor her daughter's, who was driving the car.

Elisa Merchant was forty-one when she died. A white Ford pickup came barreling through the intersection, never slowed down, and hit Elisa's car broadside on the driver's side. Elisa had died at the scene.

Lila, her mother, escaped with very minor injuries.

On the outside.

But reading about the horrible accident, Winnie saw a flash again: of Lila Merchant lying in bed in her faded lavender nightgown, curled in on herself with her arms crossed over her belly. She was crying. Sobbing.

Winnie could see what looked like a hard, dark burgundy ball in the center of Lila's abdomen. Almost as if old blood had congealed there and remained.

Lila's legs were drawn up and the top of her body curled forward around the burgundy ball. It was a posture Winnie thought of as guarding.

Then the image faded away, leaving Winnie with a deep and weighty sadness on behalf of Lila Merchant. How hard it must have been. How desperately hard. No wonder the woman had aged so much in such a short time.

Winnie looked again at the article still open on her computer screen. Lila Merchant's injuries had been minor. Some cuts to her face from flying glass, and a sprained wrist from when she braced her hand against the dashboard.

No mention of any abdominal or spinal injuries. No injuries to Lila's legs.

Winnie pictured her again, the frail old woman bent at the waist, walking so slowly while balancing on her cane.

Winnie had an idea, but she wasn't certain she was right. A true medical intuitive might be able to diagnose the problem with more confidence.

For now, she filed the idea away in the storehouse of her mind. If she was right, her mind would let her know in time.

Like toast popping out of a toaster, she described it to Amanda Birkauer. The way an idea would arrive suddenly in her mind, fully cooked.

Winnie had no such ideas about the students in the Dance department. Whatever was plaguing them and depleting their strength, whatever was making them sick and tired, Winnie still didn't have a clue.

She glanced over at Clover, so merrily chewing away.

Winnie had made carrot cake, Joe's favorite, for his birthday. She shut down her computer, went to the kitchen and cut herself a generous slice, and joined Clover on the couch for her own chew.

The dog readjusted herself to lie right up against Winnie's hip. The howling wind outside made the house seem cold. Winnie was grateful for Clover's warmth.

She thought of Lila Merchant again. The way she lay in her bed sobbing.

Sobbing and missing her daughter, Winnie was willing to bet. The accident that killed her was just over a year ago, in March. Too short a time for the grief to mend.

Joe had been gone for three years now, and Winnie still felt the pang of missing him more days than not. Especially on special days like today.

One of her former colleagues in the Psychology department specialized in grief. He called grief a "clean wound." There was no going back, no changing the outcome, no bargaining with death. A life was here one moment, and not the next.

He devised a five-step course to help the grief-stricken to move forward. Winnie had found his methods unnecessarily cold.

But she thought of that phrase now: *a clean wound.*

The hard burgundy ball inside Lila Merchant's abdomen did not look clean. It looked inflamed and infected, like a festering wound.

Was that the true cause of Lila Merchant's drastic physical change? If so, was there anything Winnie could do to help her?

A text pinged on Winnie's cell phone. She pulled it from her sweatpants pocket and read the screen.

How did it go today? Amanda Birkauer texted.

Winnie scoffed and texted her back.

Did you know about Lila Merchant's condition?

Yes.

Why didn't you tell me?

Winnie's cell phone rang.

"Because you told me you don't like to know anything before you enter the room," Amanda said.

Winnie sighed. Her friend was right.

In their years of working together in the parapsychology research lab, Winnie had learned that she performed better if she had no idea what the day's experiment would be.

"Surprise me," she told Amanda early in their

collaboration. "I don't want any bias to affect the results."

Winnie had to admit that if Amanda had told her what to expect when she saw Lila Merchant, she might have made assumptions that could have clouded her perception.

"So what did you think?" Amanda asked her now.

"Very sad," Winnie said.

"The students or Lila Merchant?"

"The students are a puzzle," Winnie said. "I'm going to interview more of them tomorrow. But Lila ... that poor woman."

"See anything?" Amanda asked.

"A very damaged aura," Winnie said. "And a few other images. I'm still trying to piece them together."

She understood Amanda's curiosity, but Winnie felt protective of Lila's grief.

And besides, Lila Merchant was a client now. Or at least the Dance department was. Winnie was careful to preserve the privacy of her clients. Once she was hired, she kept most of the details to herself.

Unless she needed Amanda's help.

"Are you sure we shouldn't ask someone like Judith to meet with her?" Winnie asked. Judith was one of the parapsychology research lab's most reliable medical intuitives.

"Remember," Amanda said, "Lila Merchant isn't

asking for help for herself. She's only hired you to find out what's wrong with her students. If you happen to help her along the way ... well, I can't see the harm, can you?"

"You're very crafty, Dr. Birkauer."

"I am."

The two of them chatted a few minutes more, then Amanda had to return to the paper she was writing for an upcoming conference. Winnie had enjoyed the research and writing aspect of her own career, but she didn't miss the pressing deadlines.

Winnie turned off her phone, then kicked off her fleece-lined slippers and sat cross-legged on the couch with her wool socked feet tucked underneath her thighs. She rested her left hand on Clover's warm back. The dog was napping again. Winnie could feel Clover's soft snoring rumbling from the top of her lungs.

Winnie breathed deeply, too, and intentionally cleared her mind.

People misunderstood clairvoyance. They thought it meant that someone like Winnie could see everything, all the time.

But her clairvoyance was a mental tool, in the same way that some people could multiply long strings of numbers in their heads. Nikola Tesla was said to be able to create his inventions mentally first, testing their flaws and imagining every component, so that by the time he built his machines in the physical world, they already worked perfectly.

Even after sixty-eight years of living with her clairvoyant mind, Winnie constantly practiced to know it better.

It was one of the reasons she volunteered as a test subject at Amanda Birkauer's lab. Amanda and her associates devised experiments that Winnie couldn't have conducted on her own, and that showed her what her clairvoyance could do.

Amanda sometimes recruited colleagues from different parts of the world to assist in various tests. In one, a woman in India held up a sign at the appointed time, and Winnie had to find her, after being given only her name, and then read the letters on her sign.

Winnie didn't understand the Hindi alphabet, but she could copy the symbols that she saw. Ten minutes later, the colleague sent Amanda a photograph of the sign, showing that Winnie had copied it exactly.

After years of practice and experimentation, Winnie had come to think of her gift as a pair of binoculars. They helped her filter out the entire, vast landscape of people and events, and allowed her to narrowly focus on a specific person, place, or thing.

Sometimes her mind made that decision for her, offering Winnie flashes of images to give her information. But Winnie could also direct that focus when she wanted to, and she directed her focus now.

After a few minutes of soft, steady breathing, a sequence of images appeared in Winnie's mind. Soon she was watching a mental movie of last Friday's exhibition performance at the College of Dance.

There was Daphne, wearing classic flesh-colored tights and a black leotard, with her long blonde hair braided and secured in loops against her scalp. She stood in the shadows just outside the bright lights of a stage.

Her friend Carmen stood beside her, dressed the same way, and nervously nibbling at her fingernail.

Daphne rose onto the toes of her ballet slippers. Warming up. Her legs were long and lithe with muscular calves. Dancers might seem so light they could float above the earth, but Winnie understood the strength that allowed them to cast that illusion.

Beside Daphne and Carmen stood two other girls and a young man, all waiting together in the wings. Now Winnie could see a male professor standing in front of a microphone on stage, welcoming the audience to the evening's exhibition.

One of the other girls now reached out to squeeze Daphne's arm. Daphne turned to her and the girl smiled. She was smaller than Daphne and Carmen and looked younger than she must have been, more like a high schooler than a young woman in college. She wore her ash-blonde hair short in a pixie cut.

Daphne nodded vaguely to the girl and turned back to listen to the professor on stage, but the ash-blonde girl tapped her on the shoulder and leaned over to whisper.

She continued talking to Daphne as the audience clapped and the professor left the stage carrying his microphone stand.

Winnie could hear music begin to play. Daphne closed her eyes and took a deep breath. The ash-blonde girl said something more, and squeezed Daphne's arm and gave her a smile, then Daphne moved elegantly onto the stage.

But rather than choosing to watch Daphne's disastrous fall, Winnie's mind shifted to a different sight.

Carmen, tall and dark-haired and dignified, glanced with disgust at the ash-blonde girl. Carmen took a few steps away from her to stand alone, deeper in the shadows.

Winnie focused on Carmen's face as the young woman glared at the ash-blonde girl. As though she could barely stand to be around her any longer.

What had the smaller girl said to Daphne that made Carmen look at her that way?

Maybe there was a clue there. Winnie bookmarked that moment in her mind.

And then she heard the audience gasp. An audible intake of their collective breath, before people starting crying out in alarm.

Winnie still looked at Carmen and the other girl. Both of them registered shock and even horror on their faces.

The ash-blonde girl covered her mouth with both hands. Carmen pushed past her and raced out onto the stage.

The male professor who had announced the performance had gotten there first. Winnie could see Daphne lying on the wooden floor in agony.

Winnie had seen enough. Her mind let her go. She came back to awareness of her own cozy living room and the softly snoring dog at her side.

Winnie remained on the couch for some time, reviewing what she saw. She might not always know why her mind showed her exactly what it did, but Winnie trusted that the information was both accurate and important.

The ash-blonde girl was the key, somehow. Although Winnie couldn't imagine why. The girl had seemed friendly and supportive, not sinister in any way.

And yet Carmen didn't trust her for some reason. Why?

Winnie could feel her internal clock starting to wind down for the night. She had done enough for one day.

Still, she couldn't resist checking her email one more time. There was a message from Lila Merchant telling her about the interviews she had set up with students for the following day.

Winnie scanned the list of seven names. Sometimes just seeing a name could give her a flash of an image.

But nothing came to her mind at the moment. Winnie turned off her computer and prepared to turn in for the night.

As she stood in the shower, the name popped into her mind. *Audrey.* The ash-blonde girl's name was Audrey.

But that hadn't been one of the names on Lila Merchant's list. She wasn't one of the students experiencing symptoms.

Winnie turned her phone back on and emailed Lila from her bedroom.

I need to talk to Audrey, too. Please add her to your list.

She wondered what Lila Merchant would think of the request. How did Winnie know the ash-blonde girl's name?

But Winnie didn't doubt that information for a moment.

Although she still had no explanation for why the girl was important.

4

Dizzy.

Nauseous.

Sleepy.

Weak.

Six different students reported similar symptoms.

Lila Merchant let Winnie use a small, empty classroom to interview the students on the list. So far Winnie didn't learn anything Lila hadn't already told her.

But then late in the afternoon the door to the classroom opened again, and in walked a familiar face.

It was the young man Winnie had seen in her vision the night before. The one who had been standing with Daphne, Carmen, and Audrey in the wings before their performance.

He was a sweet and quiet young man named Jayere.

He spoke with a slight accent, maybe Middle Eastern. And he offered Winnie her first new clue.

"Was anyone talking before the performance?" Winnie asked, although she already knew that much. She had watched the ash-blonde girl whisper continuously to Daphne.

Jayere nodded. "A girl called Audrey." He made an exasperated face and shook his head. "She can *not* stop talking. Ever. No matter if we ask her to be quiet. She whispers in class, she talks during people's performances, she's like a fly buzzing around your head." He demonstrated by waving his hands at the sides of his ears.

"Could you hear what she said?" Winnie asked.

" 'Oh, you're the best!' " Jayere mimicked in a higher voice. " 'I saw you practicing and you looked so perfect! You'll be so beautiful out there!' Which sounds nice, yes?" Jayere asked Winnie in his normal voice. "It's hard to explain, but everything she says is so very irritating."

Jayere lowered his head for a moment, as though he were ashamed. Winnie could see he didn't like to criticize.

He looked back toward the closed door, as if assuring himself they were alone. Then he leaned forward and told Winnie, "No one likes her."

"Why?" Winnie asked. "Can you explain it to me exactly?"

Because she was starting to get a feeling.

There was a term for what she was thinking, but she didn't want to jump ahead too far. She was always conscious of guarding against bias.

"She's..." Jayere paused and let out a sigh. "I don't want to sound mean. She's a nice girl. She says nice things to people. But she's like gum on the bottom of your shoe. Do you understand?"

"How do you feel when you're around her?" Winnie asked.

Jayere glanced back at the door again, then answered, "Like I can't wait to get away."

As if on cue, the door to the classroom opened, and Audrey stood on the threshold.

She smiled and said, "Jayere!"

Jayere smiled back with very little enthusiasm, and then turned to Winnie and made a face that only she could see.

He stood and offered his hand to Winnie. His skin was pleasantly warm and dry. "It was good to meet you, Dr. Parsons," he said politely. Then he mouthed to Winnie, *I have to go.*

Winnie watched him choose a path toward the door that kept him several desk lengths away from Audrey. He motioned for her to take his place in front of Winnie, then once she moved, he slipped out the door.

Winnie watched the performance with great curiosity.

And she focused her perception.

She had learned to increase and decrease her ability to see auras, as though turning a dial in her mind on or off.

It had become a useful adjustment that allowed her to be among crowds of people without feeling overwhelmed by so much visual stimulation.

But now she wanted to see the colorful bands around Jayere's and Audrey's bodies.

Because Winnie had a theory.

But their interaction was too brief. Winnie couldn't get a proper read. She dampened her awareness and promised herself that she would try again at the next opportunity.

Audrey approached Winnie's chair and held out her hand and introduced herself with nearly breathless excitement. "Hello! I'm Audrey! It's so nice to meet you!" The girl's handshake was firm and unremarkable.

She was a pretty girl with small and delicate features. Her face reminded Winnie of a little mouse. Audrey wore a black scoop-necked T-shirt and black tights under a knee-length pink floral skirt. On her feet were pink polka-dot ballet flats. From a distance anyone would think the girl was cute.

Audrey sat in the chair across from Winnie and

adjusted her spine to sit with perfect posture. She crossed her feet at the ankles, and clasped her hands together in her lap.

"Ask me anything," said Audrey. "This is so exciting!"

Winnie narrowed her eyes behind her black-rimmed glasses. "What do you think I'm here for?"

"You're a doctor investigating all the strange illnesses, aren't you?" Audrey asked. "That's what everyone is saying."

Winnie made a note on her legal pad and while her head was bent, she opened her perception to the girl's aura.

A light brown band surrounded Audrey's body. There were spots of yellow and red clustered near her heart and her throat.

But Winnie was more interested in the girl's solar plexus. So far she couldn't see anything out of the ordinary.

"Have you felt ill this semester?" Winnie asked.

"Oh, no. I always feel great."

"No dizziness," Winnie said. "Not especially tired?"

"Nope!" Audrey flexed her thin bicep. "Healthy and strong!"

Winnie made a note on her pad, just as an excuse to look away. She was beginning to understand what Jayere had said.

There was something about the girl's expression that

made Winnie feel uncomfortable. Audrey's eyes seemed to bore right into Winnie's. The girl's smile was a little too intense.

Winnie was still writing notes to herself, just words to fill up a line, when she felt a touch on her wrist.

"I would love to help," Audrey said, giving Winnie's wrist a squeeze. "Please, ask me whatever you want."

Winnie set down her pen and sat back in her chair. She found she wanted a little more distance.

"All right," Winnie said. "Can you tell me what you've noticed about any of your fellow students?"

It was as though Winnie had turned on a faucet. Audrey began her monologue and was still talking six minutes later.

Winnie watched the time tick away on the clock above Audrey's head. It was a safe place to rest her eyes.

But then Audrey would lean forward and touch Winnie's hand or wrist to get her attention, and would capture Winnie's gaze in her own.

Jayere had been right: nothing that the girl said was in any way offensive. She seemed to care about everyone else in the program.

She had nothing but compliments for Daphne, Carmen, and so many of the other students. She couldn't say enough good things.

But at the same time the girl was *exhausting.* Winnie

could feel her energy lagging the longer the girl rambled on.

Winnie tried to tune out her words, to turn Audrey's voice into white noise somewhere in the background, but the girl had a way of constantly interrupting Winnie's efforts, and forcing her to listen to the ongoing drone.

Like a fly buzzing around your head. Jayere was right about that.

Like gum on the bottom of your shoe. He was right about that, too.

"Well, thank you," Winnie said, offering the girl a smile of dismissal. Winnie closed the pages of her pad.

She had been writing nonsense to herself, just to avoid Audrey's eyes. *She's still going ... I'm getting a headache ... I need coffee ... I need chocolate.*

Now she also understood what Carmen and Daphne had been discussing the day before: about someone who made Carmen grouchy, but she was trying to do better.

Winnie could understand Carmen's feelings completely. Feeling irritable and anxious to get away, then later scolding herself for being so mean.

Audrey was a nice girl. She said nice things. She seemed to mean well and wanted to help.

But there were certain people in the world who had a particular effect on others.

Winnie called them sappers.

They sapped people of energy. Sapped them of their good moods.

In extreme cases they could even make the people around them feel ill.

Nauseous. Dizzy. Weak.

Winnie had talked to a clairvoyant who was visiting Amanda's lab one day. The woman lived in Las Vegas.

She told Winnie a story about a man she watched in one of the casinos. A sapper who had been hired as a "cooler."

"So those are real?" Winnie asked. She had heard about them, but didn't know much about the arrangement.

"Oh, yeah," the woman said. "There are about four of them in Vegas right now. The casinos take turns hiring them on all the big weekends. They save a lot of money that way."

The clairvoyant told Winnie she watched one of the coolers in action. He sat at a poker table where one of the guests had been on a hot winning streak. Within ten minutes, the winner lost his confidence and not long after lost most of his chips.

"It's like watching a vacuum suck all the life out of someone," the woman said. "I could see the poker player's aura start to get sucked away. The cooler just sat there, looking like a regular guy, but there was a big hole in his aura near his solar plexus, and that's where the other guy's aura was disappearing."

Ever since that conversation, Winnie had paid special attention to the sappers she knew.

She could see them at parties, with their auras open wide, like giant mouths devouring the energy of people around them.

The sappers weren't cruel, they weren't offensive, and they probably had no idea of their effect on others.

But they were dangerous just the same.

Winnie could imagine the students trapped in class with Audrey, or having to rehearse near her day after day.

She could imagine Daphne's excitement and energy draining away as Audrey touched her and locked eyes with her and whispered incessantly in her ear.

Like a pin piercing Daphne's energy field and her aura deflating like a balloon.

Was it enough to cause an experienced dancer to fall during her grand *jeté*?

It was enough to make a gambler lose all his winnings.

It was enough to make Winnie want to hurry out of the room and go somewhere alone where she could recover.

But she had to be careful not to make up her mind.

Not until she could confirm what she suspected was true.

So instead of fleeing out of self-preservation, she walked with Audrey out into the lobby.

It was late in the day. Most of the classes were probably over. Dancers might be rehearsing somewhere or already gone home.

But Daphne and Carmen were sitting on one of the wooden benches in the lobby. Winnie had the feeling they were waiting for her.

Carmen saw Winnie first, and seemed ready to stand, but then she saw Audrey, and settled back down. Carmen nudged Daphne and said something that caused Daphne to look up at them, too. Then the girls averted their eyes as if not wanting to be seen.

But Winnie wanted Audrey to see them. In fact, she hoped that Audrey would go speak to them so Winnie could watch.

Audrey brightened at the sight of the two girls she thought were her friends. She practically skipped over to their bench.

Winnie turned up the dial on her perception and remained where she was, far enough away to see all three of them at once.

She didn't care what the girls were saying. In fact, it was easier to observe with the volume off.

Audrey smiled. She laughed. She touched Carmen's

arm. She locked eyes with Daphne and wouldn't let her go.

Audrey talked. And talked. Daphne and Carmen tried their best to endure. But Winnie could see their auras splitting open and draining away.

From the area around Audrey's solar plexus came a long gray streamer with a sharp pointed end. Like a long gray hook to reel the other girls' energy in.

While Daphne and Carmen seemed to wilt before Winnie's eyes, Audrey grew brighter and more energized by the moment.

Winnie had seen enough. She needed to rescue the unfortunate girls.

"Daphne," she called, crooking her finger. "Carmen. Can you both come with me now? I need to speak with you right away."

Carmen nodded dully, but she seemed relieved. She helped Daphne stand, and the two of them made their way slowly across the lobby.

Audrey said a cheerful goodbye, and then waved to Winnie. Then Audrey went on to wherever she was going next.

With the lobby clear again, Winnie led the two girls to the nearest bench. Carmen and Daphne sank back down again. Carmen was shaking her head.

"I try to be nice..."

"You were nice," Daphne said.

Carmen groaned. "If you say so."

Winnie gazed at them both sympathetically. Unfortunately, there wasn't much she could do.

She couldn't make Audrey drop out of the program. She couldn't ask Lila Merchant to send her away.

But she could share her knowledge, and so she did. Explaining with academic detachment what a sapper was.

Winnie could see a light go on in Carmen's eyes. "Yes," she said. "That's exactly what it's like."

Winnie was careful not to blame Audrey for Daphne's broken leg. That was going too far.

"There are some people who simply drain us," Winnie said. "It's not their fault. They're not doing it on purpose. But our bodies have a built-in emergency cord. When they want us to get away from someone, our bodies let us know."

"How?" Daphne asked.

"By making us feel sick," Winnie said. "Depleted. Grouchy," she said, looking at Carmen, "even though we can't understand why."

Carmen sighed. "I mean, it's not like she's a bad person. I get that. I just..." She shrugged. "You understand."

Daphne looked around the lobby at the few students milling about. She lowered her voice to a whisper. "So what are we supposed to do?" she asked Winnie. "Just avoid her?"

"Be aware of her effect on you and limit yourselves to just a few minutes at a time."

"Seriously?" Carmen asked. "That would do it?"

"I have sappers in my life, too," Winnie said. "Friends I'm not willing to throw away. But I learned long ago to keep our phone calls very short. And I never stay with them when I'm visiting out of town, even though they ask. It's not worth it. I don't want to get angry with them. I love them," she said with a smile, "I just can't be around them too long."

Carmen and Daphne sat in silence for a few moments and considered Winnie's advice.

"So, do they ever change?" Carmen asked. "Do they get better?"

"Sometimes," Winnie said, although she didn't add that she hadn't seen it herself. The sappers in her life were always the same. "Sometimes people notice that they don't have many close friends, and the introspective ones start to wonder why. If she ever asks you for the truth, you might find a kind way to tell her."

"If she would just stop *talking* all the time," Carmen said.

"Yes," Winnie said. "You might tell her that."

Winnie's headache had dulled, but she still wanted a

cup of coffee and some chocolate. She had both of those waiting for her at home.

"Did you have any other questions for me?" Winnie asked the girls. "I had the impression you were waiting for me before."

"Oh, we just wanted to give you this," Carmen said, pulling a dark purple flyer out of her book bag. "They rescheduled the exhibition after what happened to Daph. It's this Friday. I thought ... you might like to come."

Winnie held her hand to her heart. She felt incredibly touched. She smiled and said, "Of course I will come."

She let the girls go and promised to see them in a few days.

Then she went in search of Lila Merchant.

Coffee and chocolate could wait.

Helping Lila was more important.

5

The professor was in her office. The room was another work of art.

If the Dance building was a luxury ocean liner, Lila's office was the captain's cabin.

A thick woven rug covered most of the polished wooden floor. Lila's cherry wood desk took up most of the room. There were photographs filling the wall behind Lila's chair. Winnie assumed the elegant ballerina in all of the photos was Lila.

Now the bent old woman that ballerina had become sat in a burgundy leather chair that seemed too big for her. Winnie could see a pillow propped behind Lila's spine. She hoped it was giving the poor woman some relief.

Lila motioned for Winnie to sit in one of the soft

leather chairs across the desk. All of the furnishings made Winnie feel like she was in Lila Merchant's home, not in a university professor's office.

Winnie's own office had been more like what she thought of as the norm: ugly file cabinets, scuffed desk, second-hand chairs, piles of papers everywhere. But Lila Merchant's office was cozy and immaculate.

Winnie's gaze was drawn to the cherry wood credenza behind Lila's chair. There was a group of framed photographs there.

Photos of a little girl, a teenager, a grown woman. The same radiant smile on all of their faces.

"Your daughter," Winnie said. It was a statement, not a question.

Lila swiveled her chair around and studied the pictures.

She turned back to Winnie. "Elisa. She … died."

"I know," Winnie said. "I'm so sorry."

Tears welled in Lila Merchant's pale blue eyes. She pursed her lips together and silently nodded.

"I have your answer about the students," Winnie said. "I think it will be all right from now on. But first I want to talk to you about something else. You asked me yesterday if I saw anything—about you. I didn't then, but I can see it now."

Lila's eyes widened slightly. The unshed tears glistened at the edge of her lashes.

Her aura was still in tatters. The edges billowed in an unseen breeze.

But what Winnie could see now, as she saw in her vision the evening before, was the hard ball in Lila's abdomen, the same color as the burgundy leather chair where she sat.

"Our bodies are remarkable," Winnie said. "They obey us, whether we realize it or not. They listen to what we ask, and they try to build what it is we want."

"I don't … understand," Lila said.

"In the car accident, you sprained your wrist. But there was no damage to your spine or neck, isn't that right?"

Lila nodded. She didn't ask Winnie how she knew. She didn't accuse her of reading about the accident behind her back.

"Why do you think you're bent over now?" Winnie asked. Because sometimes people knew the truth if only someone would ask them.

"I think it's … sorrow," Lila said. "Bottomless sorrow." And this time the tears in her eyes slid down her cheeks. She brushed them away and steadied her gaze on Winnie.

Winnie had to pause before speaking again. Lila's bravery tore at her heart. She had survived the accident, and survived the death of her child, and she still wanted to mother and protect the students under her care.

Another woman in Lila's position might have given up. Given up teaching, given up living.

But Lila Merchant had found a way to contain her pain so that she could go on sharing the knowledge and the love she still had.

She had compressed it all into a hard dark ball, and she guarded it with her crooked body.

"I have a friend named Judith who is a medical intuitive," Winnie said. "She can see inside people's bodies. She works with doctors all over the country to help them diagnosis their hardest cases. Judith told me about some of the patients.

"Sometimes when people hear they have cancer," Winnie said, "their bodies build a cocoon. It can happen over a few weeks or even a few days. It's amazing. Suddenly the fascia—the connective tissue surrounding the muscles and joints—starts to multiply and harden like a thick, dense web.

"If someone knows they have breast cancer, maybe a week later they can't lift their arm anymore because the fascia has built a protective web all around that area. Judith said a man who found out he had prostate cancer built a cocoon all around his groin. Within a few weeks he could barely walk anymore because the connective tissue was so tight and dense."

"But it's all in their mind?" Lila asked.

"No," Winnie said. "Their mind is creating it, and

their body obeys. It's very real. And it's more common than I ever knew. Our bodies are always trying to help us, to protect us in whatever ways they can."

"And you think ... I've done that?"

"Not consciously," Winnie said, "but yes. I can see the burden you're holding inside. And your body thinks you want to protect it, so it..."

"Obeyed," Lila finished.

The two women sat for a moment looking at one another. Winnie didn't want to press Lila any further than she wanted to go.

Fresh tears welled in Lila's eyes. Her voice cracked as she said, "What if it's my punishment?"

"For what?" Winnie said. Her heart ached for Lila Merchant. "It wasn't your fault. None of it. And it isn't wrong that you survived."

"Isn't it?" she asked. "Why should the old outlive the young?"

"Lila, why should anything bad happen in this world, period? How can any of us understand that? But we're all doing the best we can."

Lila bowed her head and covered her eyes and let her tears wash against her fingers.

She drew in a breath that rattled like a sob, but then she was quiet and she took her time to recover.

In the silence, as she waited, Winnie thought of Joe and the cancer that took him from her. She understood sorrow and how deeply it could drag a person under.

But it was moments like this, when she thought she might help someone else, that made Winnie still feel excited with the break of each new day.

Finally Lila spoke. Her voice wavered, but she looked Winnie straight in the eyes.

"So what am I supposed to do?" she asked.

"I'd like to introduce you to my friend Judith," Winnie said. "She's an expert at deconstructing people's cocoons."

"So I might stand upright again?" Lila asked with new strength in her voice.

Winnie nodded.

Lila closed her eyes and blew out a great sigh.

She looked at Winnie again, and there was life in her pale blue eyes.

"Now tell me about the children," Lila said.

Winnie glanced at the table to her left, with the shiny silver carafe.

"Please, is that coffee?" she asked.

Lila smiled. "Let me make us a pot."

6

───────

"Dr. Parsons! You're here!"

"Hello, Audrey. Your dance was lovely."

And it was. Winnie had enjoyed all of the performances immensely.

It was rare that she went out on a Friday night. Rarer still that she had a date.

Amanda Birkauer invited herself along to see the ash-blonde girl who had caused all the trouble.

Winnie introduced the two of them and then left them alone.

She strolled to the front of the theater to congratulate Carmen and Jayere on their splendid dances.

Daphne stood nearby with her crutches jammed under her arms. But she was smiling and laughing with her friends.

"Thank you for inviting me," Winnie said. "All of you were so beautiful to watch. I'm amazed at what you can do."

"I'll get my cast off in time for the last one of the semester," Daphne said. "I hope you'll come watch me, too."

Winnie felt a glow of energy from being around the young dancers. And a glow of gratitude for being included.

She had always enjoyed being around the young people she taught. She had forgotten how lively they made her feel.

Winnie felt a light tug on her arm. She turned to her left. Lila Merchant stood beaming at her side.

Lila shifted her cane to her left hand and then swung her right arm in a circle. "I saw Judith today. Look what she already did."

Winnie had made a special call to the medical intuitive and asked her to fit Lila Merchant into her schedule as soon as she could.

Lila gripped Winnie's wrist and looked into her eyes. "Thank you. For everything. Thank you."

Winnie laid her hand over Lila's and smiled warmly at the professor. "It was my pleasure. More than you know."

Winnie left the dancers and Dr. Merchant to

socialize with others in the audience, and she made her way back to Amanda.

"All right," Amanda said, spying Winnie. "I'll have to let you go now," she told Audrey. "I still have some work to do tonight."

Audrey reached out her hand. "It was so great to meet you, Dr. Birkauer! I'd love to come to your lab some time. That sounds like so much fun!"

Audrey shook Winnie's hand, too, and then went off to join the cluster of her classmates.

"You invited her to the lab?" Winnie asked as soon as they were free.

"Of course," Amanda said. "After what you told me? I have no idea what tests I'll do, but you bet I want I want to know what makes that girl tick."

"So what did you think of her?" Winnie asked.

Amanda groaned. "Exhausting. I don't think she ever took a breath."

They stepped out of the polished wood interior of the building, to where steel and glass met together under the clear night sky.

Winnie tipped back her head to admire the sparkling stars and drew in a lungful of fresh cold air.

She zipped up her coat and pulled her fleece hat and gloves out of the pockets. She could have driven the few blocks from her house to campus, but by the time she made her way out of the parking garage, it would have been shorter just to walk.

And Amanda was always up for any kind of exercise, so the two of them set off at a brisk walk together.

Winnie had made banana bread that morning. Amanda could never say no to that.

And a certain dog would be thrilled with the celebrity guest. Clover had no idea what was about to happen.

"Do you think you can teach Audrey how not to be a sapper?" Winnie asked. "Carmen and Daphne asked me if people like that ever change."

"Doubt it," Amanda said. "We all are what we are. But I guess we can find out if I can come up with the right experiment."

Winnie strode beneath the neighborhood lights. She could tell that Amanda was shortening her athletic stride to keep at Winnie's slower pace.

It was what friends did, and Winnie appreciated it. And she enjoyed any time when she and Amanda could get together and have more than one of their hurried conversations.

"So," Winnie said, "how many sappers would you say you know?"

"Top of my head? At least ten I can name right now. My mother, for one."

"Oh," Winnie said, "I forgot about her. Would you ever tell any of them?"

Amanda answered immediately, "Absolutely not."

Winnie laughed at how emphatic she was. "Why not?"

"Because what if *I'm* the sapper and they've all just been waiting for a chance to tell me? Can't risk it. I'd rather not know."

"I would tell you," Winnie said.

"Of course you would, heartless."

Winnie laughed. Then she lengthened her stride so Amanda could walk faster.

It was what friends did.

THE SLIP OF A RIB

1

Winnie Parsons stood at the granite-topped island in her kitchen and pressed her palms into a soft round lump of dough. She had awakened in the mood for bread. Not just for the taste of it, but mostly for the smell of a yeasty loaf baking in the oven, warming the whole house.

A cold February morning like today made her want to stay inside, bake, eat, sit by the fire with a mug of coffee or hot chocolate, and read. Her yellow Labrador, Clover, had different ideas of what was fun, and so Winnie had walked her on the nearby University of Arizona campus first to let the dog frolic on the frost-covered grass.

But now Clover was curled up on her dog bed beside the crackling fire, and Winnie could fulfill her urge to bake. There were a few steps between here and a hot, finished loaf, but Winnie's part in it was short. Just mix a few ingredients, knead, then let the dough sit covered by a dishtowel all day in the warmth of the kitchen window. Even in winter, the sun shone through golden onto one particular spot on the counter. The dough would be ready to bake by midafternoon.

Winnie's cell phone rang. Her hands were still deep in dough. She might have let the call go to voicemail, if not for the name she saw on her screen.

She used her relatively clean pinky finger to press the button to put the call on her phone's speaker.

Dr. Amanda Birkauer was usually in a hurry, and this morning was no exception.

"Got an interesting call just now," said Amanda without any greeting or other preamble. Winnie didn't mind. She liked her friend's ability to cut right to it, leave out the fluff, get to the interesting parts sooner.

Amanda had been Winnie's colleague in the University of Arizona Psychology department when Winnie was a professor there. Winnie—Dr. Winifred Parsons—had retired four years ago, but her decades-long friendship with Amanda endured.

They had another connection as well. Amanda Birkauer was the Assistant Director of the university's mind lab, also known as the parapsychology research lab.

Winnie was a frequent test subject there. As a clairvoyant and occasional medical intuitive, Winnie wanted both to share her knowledge and to learn more about her gifts herself. She thought of them as any talent, like the ability to play chess or to do the high jump. She had been born clairvoyant, but she could still grow and improve the more she practiced.

And the more she learned from Amanda's scientists and from other psychics who visited the lab, the more Winnie understood what she might be capable of if she expanded what she thought of as even possible.

"Remember Penny Bristol?" Amanda asked.

Winnie smoothed her dough into a ball and thought for a moment. "No." But as soon as she said it, an image flashed in her mind: of an elderly woman, well-dressed and obviously wealthy, pushing a rolling walker that had a cargo basket on top. A soft blue blanket lined the basket, and a small brown and white dog rode nestled inside.

"King Arthur!" Winnie said, smiling.

"The one," Amanda confirmed over the speaker.

It must have been five or six years ago. Mrs. Penny Bristol had brought her Cavalier King Charles Spaniel, named King Arthur, to the parapsychology research lab to see if anyone could read the little dog's mind.

Winnie had been on her way out of one of the

rooms where she'd participated in whatever new test Amanda and her lab assistants had cooked up for her that day.

Winnie came to a sudden halt in front of the woman and her dog. She hadn't planned on stopping—she had her own work to do, and needed to get back to her office—but something about the dog tugged at her and made her want to stay.

"Well, hello there." Winnie smiled at the spaniel and reached out to pet its soft head between the two long ears that hung over the lip of the basket.

The dog growled at Winnie and bared his small teeth.

"Arthur! Stop that!" Mrs. Bristol seemed embarrassed. "He's normally never like this," she said by way of apology. And then tears misted her eyes. "I ... I don't know what to do with him. Something has happened. He's not himself anymore."

A phrase had come to Winnie's mind. A phrase and an image.

"He has a rib out," Winnie told Mrs. Bristol. "On his left side. He's been in terrible pain for over a week. He's sorry, but he hasn't known how else to tell you."

Mrs. Bristol gaped at Winnie. "How ... how..."

Winnie waved the question away. "If you take him to your vet this morning, I'm sure they can fix it right away."

Mrs. Bristol had gripped Winnie's hand. "Thank you, oh thank you!"

Amanda came out of the lab then just in time to see the end of their conversation. Winnie gave her a nod, then hurried off toward the stairs leading up to her floor.

"Who was that?" Mrs. Bristol asked.

"I'm sorry," Winnie could hear Amanda tell the woman, "but we keep our test subjects' identities confidential."

Winnie was there that morning in her capacity as Test Subject number 2143, not as Professor Winifred Parsons.

She appreciated Amanda's discretion. Most of Winnie's colleagues had no idea she was clairvoyant. Winnie suspected that many of them would not handle it well. Although the university's mind lab was well-respected among others pursuing that same research, some scientists still viewed parapsychology as a fringe subject, not worthy of serious study—and even less worthy of funding.

Winnie had already risen high through the ranks of the Psychology department by then, even acting as Chair of the department for a while. She wrote many well-respected articles and textbooks in her field of Consumer Psychology. Her students and colleagues thought of her as a typical academic.

So although Winnie was happy to help Mrs. Bristol and King Arthur solve their problem in the moment, she did not want to see them up on her own floor, Mrs. Bristol smiling in her office doorway, loudly thanking her for reading the little dog's mind.

And besides, Winnie hadn't read the dog's mind. That wasn't how she received the information. Instead she saw a flashed image of the misplaced rib, and heard a phrase in her own voice telling her everything else she conveyed to Mrs. Bristol.

"So what do the two of them need now?" Winnie asked Amanda.

"Nothing," Amanda said. "Penny Bristol died about three months ago—"

"Oh, I'm sorry to hear that."

"—and believe it or not, she left you some money."

"She *what*?"

Amanda chuckled. "Not by name. That's why I got the call this morning. Someone at the Animal Adoption Center wanted to know who that nice white-haired lady was who told Mrs. Bristol that King Arthur had slipped a rib."

Winnie's hair was more of a natural blondish-white, but she didn't mind the description. The hair had made her look older than her years for at least a decade. Now at sixty-eight, Winnie knew that when strangers looked at her they saw an old lady. She sometimes used that to her advantage to fade unnoticed into a crowd.

"Apparently Penny left most of her money to the Animal Adoption Center. Isn't that nice?"

"It is," Winnie agreed. She thought well of anyone who used their wealth to take care of children and animals in particular.

"She also gave them a separate twenty thousand dollars specifically to spend on *you*."

"On me? Why?"

Winnie set her dough in a bowl, covered it with a clean dish towel, and positioned the bowl on the counter beneath the sunny kitchen window.

She quickly washed the flour from her hands, then took Amanda off speaker. Winnie was tired of shouting.

She took the phone to the bedroom to retrieve her headset for a more comfortable call. Then she returned to the living room and sat on the thick Asian rug next to Clover, leaning against the warm fireplace hearth.

"Don't make me drag it out of you," Winnie said. "Just start at the beginning."

"Hold on."

Winnie could hear Amanda cover the phone with her hand and speak to someone who had come into her office. Winnie was always amazed at Amanda's ability to juggle so many demands at once: teaching, running the lab, and writing new academic articles every few months to share her lab's findings with the international scientific community.

Amanda was fifty-three, a full fifteen years younger than Winnie, but even in her twenties and thirties, Winnie never had Amanda's kind of energy or her ability to multitask.

And in Amanda's spare time, what there was of it, she trained as a tri-athlete. Winnie certainly never had that much extra energy to burn.

Some people were just made differently. Winnie enjoyed watching her friend manage her busy life and career, but she preferred watching it from the quiet and calm of her own slower life.

Like right now. Winnie added another log to the fire, then settled back next to Clover. She petted the dog and patiently waited for Amanda to return to the call. The dog groaned as Winnie scratched behind her ears, then Clover sank even more deeply into her plush green bed.

"Sorry," Amanda said. "I have to go in a sec. Here's the short version. Penny gave them twenty thousand to spend on that nice white-haired psychic lady from the U of A if they ever need to solve any behavioral issues. You're supposed to be the pet guru now, I guess."

"I don't mean to sound ungrateful," Winnie said, "but don't you think they should call Chandra instead?" Winnie had met the woman several years before at

Amanda's lab. Chandra actually was an intuitive pet communicator.

"She specifically left the money for you," Amanda said. "It's in her will. The Animal Adoption Center is emailing me a copy any minute."

Winnie sighed. "Okay, so what do I do?"

"They need you. They're doing a Valentine's Weekend Adopt-a-thon, and they want to place as many animals as they can."

"But that's this weekend," Winnie said. "Awfully short notice."

"I think it took them a while to figure out how to find you. But it sounds like now they're desperate. Some of their animals are pretty shut down. They're hoping you can come out there and find out what all of them need so the Center can get them to their forever homes. Sounds pretty sweet, actually."

"It does," Winnie agreed. Although the responsibility of the task seemed daunting. How many animals needed her help? What if she couldn't hear them? And how was she supposed to get this done by the weekend?

Amanda told someone on her end, "Okay, I'm coming. Listen," she said to Winnie, "gotta go. I'll send you over the will later if you want it. But the person who wants you is a woman named Irma Makelski. I'll send you her info. Good luck. See you."

"See you—"

The call ended as abruptly as it started.

Winnie removed her headset and continued to sit on the floor beside Clover, running her fingers through the dog's thick winter coat.

She didn't know what to think.

On the one hand, she was touched that that short interaction so many years ago had made Mrs. Bristol remember Winnie in her will.

On the other hand, Winnie couldn't be certain that she would be able to communicate with any of the other animals at the shelter. It was not a skill she practiced. She didn't even speak with Clover that way. The two of them had a close relationship, but Clover spoke with her eyes and her wagging tail, not by sending Winnie images and messages.

Although maybe it was only because Winnie never tried to reach out to her that way.

She closed her eyes. Took a deep and clearing breath. Then she opened her eyes and watched for Clover's reaction as Winnie spoke in her mind to the dog.

Clover. Are you a pretty girl?

The dog continued to sleep.

Clover, do you want a carrot?

That got the Lab to open one eye.

Clover, do you want to—

Winnie had been about to ask her if she wanted to

go for a walk.

But the wind was howling and the thermometer showed it was in the forties outside, and Winnie didn't want to lie to the dog. She would not be taking Clover for a walk again today, even if it promising that might prove she could talk to the dog in her mind.

Winnie let the sleeping dog sleep. She heard her email ding.

Before running out the door to whatever demand was pulling on her next, Amanda had taken a moment to forward Winnie the will.

Winnie skipped through the formal language at the beginning, and scanned through the pages looking for the part that mentioned her.

But her eyes settled on Section 6, first. It bore the title PROVISIONS FOR THE HEALTH AND HAPPINESS OF KING ARTHUR.

So the little dog had outlived his mistress. Winnie knew that could be a tricky situation. She had already made her niece Rose swear that she and her family would adopt Clover if Winnie should exit before the dog. It gave her great peace of mind.

Mrs. Bristol had obviously sought that peace of mind as well.

Her will appointed a woman named Charlotte Amper to be King Arthur's caretaker. And Mrs. Bristol left the Amper woman a generous salary and expense allowance to see that it was properly done.

Section 6 of the will listed all the various services that should be paid for out of the estate. The list was long, but a few of them caught Winnie's eye.

Weekly grooming by someone named Pierre LeFranc, at a rate easily three times as much as Winnie spent on her own haircuts. Continued employment of the cook, Margery, who knew how to make all of the spaniel's favorite foods. Gas and upkeep for Mrs. Bristol's Cadillac so that Charlotte Amper could drive King Arthur through the foothills above Tucson and let him enjoy looking at the scenery out the window.

Winnie scrolled down to the next page where Section 6 of the will continued. When it came to her beloved dog's comfort, Mrs. Bristol had obviously tried to think of everything.

In a paragraph titled *House,* her lawyer had written a brief explanation of what his client intended. Mrs. Bristol did not want King Arthur's life to be any more upended than it would already be after his owner's death.

Therefore the executor of the estate should delay selling the house and distributing the proceeds to the designated charity. Instead, Mrs. Bristol wanted Charlotte Amper and the dog to stay in the house with all expenses paid for as long as King Arthur lived.

Suddenly Winnie didn't feel so strange about the twenty thousand dollars Mrs. Bristol had allocated to her. Instead she took it in stride.

Mrs. Bristol saw her as part of the team, along with Pierre the groomer and Margery the cook and Charlotte Amper the dog caretaker. That white-haired psychic lady had a role to play, too.

If Mrs. Bristol wanted the Animal Adoption Center to have the resources it needed to help place more of their animals in loving homes, then Winnie was happy to help the cause.

A Valentine's Weekend Adopt-a-thon was exactly the kind of charitable event Winnie could feel good about supporting.

Now she only hoped she could justify Mrs. Bristol's faith in what Winnie could do.

2

Winnie had never visited the Animal Adoption Center. She often told herself that when the time came to get a dog or cat, she would go to the shelter and rescue the one that felt like the right match.

But the years went by, and Winnie was always too busy at work to think about bringing home a pet. She kept pushing the matter to some vague time in the future.

Her husband, Joe, had solved that by bringing home a puppy for Winnie for her sixty-first birthday. It was love at first sight. How Joe knew which puppy to choose was as much a mystery to him as it was to Winnie. Clover slipped so perfectly into their family life, it was as though she were a puzzle piece that had been missing.

Joe died just four years later. Although Winnie still missed him every day, she could only imagine how bottomlessly lonely she might have felt if she didn't still have Clover to share her life.

So although she had never followed through on her plan to visit the Animal Adoption Center, she was glad to pull up to the building now and be able to help the animals inside find homes with people who would love them the rest of their lives.

The Center was set far back from the road, so Winnie couldn't see its bright orange exterior until she drove further up the gravel driveway.

The building looked freshly painted. Maybe some of Penny Bristol's money had been spent that way. The Center must have hired an artist, too, because painted on top of the orange backdrop was a cheerful mural of dogs and cats and birds all playing together.

This was not the solemn, prison-like facility Winnie dreaded seeing. Her heart immediately lightened.

From where she parked, Winnie could see a large chain link enclosure at the back of the property. It might be as big as the building complex itself. Groups of dogs ran and played on an imitation grass surface out there, supervised by several people who must be on the staff.

Winnie entered the building, where the brightly painted colors continued inside the lobby. Each brick wall bore a different cheerful color: yellow, turquoise, sky blue, pink.

There were framed photographs covering most of the turquoise wall. Winnie could see happy individuals and happy families hugging the pets they had adopted from the Center.

Whoever designed the look of the place knew how to make it welcoming for the visitors. From what Winnie saw so far, this did not feel like a shelter where people dumped their unwanted animals. It felt more like a boarding facility where pets waited for the right people to come along who would then whisk them off to their proper and loving homes.

A young woman in her early twenties, with shoulder-length purple hair, sat behind a front reception counter talking into a telephone headset. Winnie wondered if she colored her hair specifically to add to the cheerful ambience of the lobby. The young woman smiled at Winnie and held up a finger for her to wait while she answered a few more of the caller's questions.

As soon as the call ended, the young woman said, "Welcome! Are you here to find a pet?"

"No, actually, I'm here for an appointment with Irma."

The girl's eyes lit with excitement. "Are you that psychic?"

Winnie preferred less flashy terms—clairvoyant,

gifted, intuitive—but she understood that people grouped all psi abilities into the same broad category. The word *psychic* had taken its hits over the years, especially when dial-a-psychic ads started appearing on late-night TV. Unfortunately, there were many frauds out there who were happy to take people's money in exchange for vague pronouncements.

Someone close to you will be sick. A good guess. Everyone knew someone who succumbed to at least the common cold.

You will face unexpected difficulties in the new year, but by summer, they should all work out.

I see more, but I'm afraid our time is up. Input your credit card for another five minutes.

Winnie used to wonder how the fake psychics could live with themselves. How they could prey on other people's hopes and fears.

But her years studying psychology had put that mystery to rest. Some people were simply greedy. Some people thought if they could trick other people, it meant they were smarter than everyone else.

They didn't care who they hurt in the process. Feeling guilty never even crossed their minds.

Winnie confirmed to the purple-haired receptionist who she was. The young woman jumped up from her chair and went off through a door to her right to find Irma Makelski somewhere in back.

In that brief moment while the door was open, Winnie could hear the noise that the thick brick walls so effectively screened.

Dogs barking. And barking. Some howling. Human voices shouting over the din.

The door closed again and Winnie shivered. She could hear pain in that barking and howling.

Despite the carefully managed exterior, this place was a shelter after all. Animals had been dumped here by their thoughtless owners. Animals had been captured and brought in from the streets.

So far, the animals here had missed out on a pampered life like King Arthur's. But maybe Winnie could help them find new owners who would shower them with that kind of love.

The door behind the reception desk opened again, and a tall, thin woman with short gray hair came striding into the lobby with her hand outstretched and a smile on her weathered face.

"Mrs. Parsons."

It was Doctor Parsons, but Winnie rarely corrected people about that, either. She smiled and shook the woman's hand. "Winnie, please."

"Irma. I'm so glad you're here. Thank you for coming."

The director of the Animal Adoption Center might be Winnie's age or older. It was difficult for Winnie to tell. She had the leathery skin of someone who spent a lifetime outdoors. Winnie liked her plain and unfussy look.

The short gray hair, no makeup, no jewelry. This woman was practical and was here to work. Irma wore jeans that might have been clean at some point, but that were currently covered in dust and crusted food and what looked like a few spots of dried blood.

She wore an oversized light blue sweatshirt that bore the Animal Adoption Center logo, a circle with a floppy-eared, grinning dog in the center. It was one of the faces from the mural on the front of the building.

Despite the dirt and stains on it, the sweatshirt looked fairly new. Maybe staff clothing was another benefit of Penny Bristol's bequest. Remembering how elegantly Mrs. Bristol was dressed the day Winnie met her, Winnie had the feeling that Mrs. Bristol would approve.

Winnie was dressed just as casually as Irma. She wore long john bottoms underneath her charcoal gray hiking pants, one of Joe's old T-shirts beneath a coral-colored fleece sweater, and her purple fleece vest over that in case they would spend time outdoors and she needed to keep warm. On her feet she wore what she usually wore outside the house, a pair of comfortable and sturdy sneakers.

"Dog?" Irma asked, picking a few of Clover's yellow

hairs off the shoulder of Winnie's dark purple vest. She studied the sample. "Labrador?"

Winnie laughed. "Oh, you're good."

"Since you're already a dog owner," Irma said, "you probably understand what you're in for here." She pointed to the various stains on her jeans and sweatshirt. "Fancy Feast, slobber, dog vomit, blood from a broken toenail." She brushed off the back of her jeans. "Who knows what else. Can't be too fussy."

Irma smiled with radiant warmth. Winnie liked her immediately.

She opened her vision to see Irma's aura. A beautiful aqua with pale bands of silver shimmering around some of her joints.

"Ready?" Irma asked her.

Winnie dimmed her clairvoyant vision again. She suddenly felt nervous. What was she about to hear, see, and feel?

Would the fear and misery of some of these animals overwhelm Winnie once she passed through the reception door?

Irma clasped Winnie's right arm. It was a friendly and steadying gesture. Then the two of them stepped back into the belly of the shelter.

3

The main square footage of the expansive building was divided into different areas with their own separate hallways. Rows of kennels lined the hallway on the right and left. Winnie walked through that first gauntlet with Irma still clasping her arm.

"We'll start with the dogs," Irma said. "These are just some of them."

"How many animals do you have in all?" Winnie asked.

"A little over three hundred."

Winnie's heart gave a nervous jump. This was Tuesday. The Valentine Adopt-a-thon started on Friday.

How on earth was she going to get to all of them by then?

"Most of them are dogs," Irma said, "but about a

third are cats. And we have some parrots and other birds. We'll get to them last."

Winnie nodded, still feeling slightly stunned. Irma seemed to sense her hesitation.

"Oh, and I wanted to make sure you know that you'll get your money at the end of the week. It's just sitting in our account with the rest of Penny Bristol's donation."

Winnie had sent Irma her fee schedule the day before. Winnie's experience in Consumer Psychology taught her long ago that people only value what they pay for. She charged lawyer-like prices for her consultation work, knowing it would help her clients trust and follow her advice.

But this was the first time she would be billing against a retainer fund, just like a lawyer.

A few days' work would barely dent the twenty thousand dollars in that retainer. But Winnie was glad to know the money was already there, and that it would in no way deplete what Mrs. Bristol had already generously left for the Center.

And, Winnie reminded herself, in a way she, too, was a gift to the Center. She was here to help them sort out any of the animals' behavioral problems so that as many of them as possible could be adopted over the upcoming weekend.

"Ready?" Irma asked as they stood at the head of the two rows of kennels.

Winnie nodded. At least this should be interesting. Other than yesterday's brief experiment with Clover, she had never deliberately tried to communicate with animals before.

She began by opening her heart. By sending out love to the dogs she was about to meet.

My name is Winnie, she told them. *I am here to help you. Please tell me what I can do for you to make your lives better.*

A rush of sound boomed into Winnie's ears. The dogs were barking, some of them whining their high-pitched whines.

But the sounds weren't only outside her body, they were inside her mind, crowding to get her attention.

Winnie covered her ears with her hands. Then she shut down her internal hearing, the way she had trained herself to stop seeing the auras of everyone around her in a crowd. It was a form of self-preservation. Too much sensory stimulation would quickly exhaust her body and mind.

"Are you all right?" Irma asked her.

Winnie answered with a wry smile. "Just a little mistake," she confessed. Then she said out loud to the dogs in the room, "One at a time will be much easier. I promise I'll get to all of you."

Irma raised her eyebrows. But she let Winnie continue without asking any distracting questions.

They began walking slowly past each of the kennels. Dogs rushed to the fronts of their wire cages, some of them barking, some wagging, some whimpering.

The sound of their voices echoed off the concrete walls and floor. But Winnie did her best to ignore the physical noise and to concentrate instead on the images and phrases streaming into her mind.

Some clairvoyants received information as though complete knowledge packets had been downloaded into their minds. Some relied on reading emotions. A few even received smells.

Winnie had always seen flashes of images that told her what she needed to know. She was also an auditory clairvoyant who heard words and phrases, spoken in her own voice inside her mind.

One of the continuing series of experiments at Amanda Birkauer's lab was to identify all the ways those with psi gifts received their knowledge of events past, present, and future.

Winnie paid close attention now to how she communicated with these animals. She would report all of it to Amanda later.

Hello, she told the dogs as she walked slowly past each kennel on the left and right. *I see you. Hello!* She silently greeted each of them as if they were coming up to her at a dog park.

But there were so many of them. Winnie was still

having difficulty separating the individuals from just the mass of striving energies within that room.

Although most of the dogs stood at the fronts of their kennels waiting to be seen and greeted, Winnie noticed that a few of them stayed pressed against the back corners of their enclosures, either too afraid or too dejected to come to the front.

These were the ones who needed her most. But she couldn't rush them to try to open up. Winnie would have to take her time. Just meeting all the dogs in this one section of the Center might require the rest of the morning.

She didn't want to worry about how long it might take. So she addressed it openly with Irma. "I might not get to all of them before Friday, you know. But I'll come here every day this week and next week, and however long I need to."

Irma smiled with relief. "Good. Thank you. We'll do our best. I'm sure it will be fine."

As Winnie continued walking slowly between the two rows, a phrase popped into her mind.

No one wants me.

Because the phrase came to her in Winnie's own voice, she didn't know which dog had sent it. She looked at the nearest dogs' faces, hoping to feel some connection.

One of them, a large white dog with a thick, fluffy

coat and huge paws, stood at the front of his kennel wagging his tail. He met Winnie's gaze and panted in happy greeting. He was too joyful to have sent her that message.

She scanned the other kennels, but none of the other dogs seemed to reach out. Winnie gave up trying so hard to hear, and went back to slowly walking between the two rows.

When she and Irma reached the end of the long hall, Winnie stood against a closed door and surveyed the room.

Irma's staff kept the place clean. The shiny concrete floor looked like it was frequently mopped. The insides of the kennels looked free of any puddles of urine or piles of waste. Fresh bowls of water had been set out for all of the dogs. They each had a towel where they could curl up to find some warmth and a little cushioning from the hard concrete floor. Winnie suspected this was as nice of a shelter as any.

But as orderly as it was, as clean as Irma and her staff kept it, no amount of soap or bleach could hide what Winnie smelled.

It was a pungent, grimy odor that made her want to cover her nose with her hand. A smell of anguish. That was the only way she could think of it.

To be cooped up in these kennels, day after day,

night after night—how would these poor dogs interpret what had happened?

Maybe some of them used to live in houses with soft rugs or beds to lie on. Maybe some of them spent every day in a dusty back yard, or even tied to a stake with a chain.

Maybe some of them had never lived with humans, but had grown up fending for themselves as strays.

Winnie closed her eyes. Did she really want to know?

But Penny Bristol had asked her to do this. Penny Bristol wanted Winnie to help.

"Okay," Winnie said, more to herself than to Irma. "Let's go again. Kennel by kennel."

And this time, she could see them more clearly, dog by dog. They weren't just a mass of unfortunate animals all crowded in together.

Winnie cleared her mind. She told her sharpened senses this was all right. She remembered why she was here and what she hoped to do.

"Do you want to write this down?" Winnie asked.

Irma scrambled out through the closed door and quickly returned with a notepad and pen.

And finally Winnie could feel her mind settle in. She stopped blocking the information that wanted to come to her. Suddenly the images and words came flooding into her head. She realized she knew more about these animals than she believed she could when she first entered the room.

"Felix," Winnie said, pointing to the shepherd mix on her right. "Likes cats, especially gray ones. There was one like that in the house where he was raised.

"Precious," she said, pointing to the middle-aged chihuahua shivering at the back of her kennel. "Kicked by the father of the family. Broken leg that they never took her to the vet for. She needs someone kind who just wants to love her and baby her."

"Are you sure?" Irma asked, lifting her pen from the notepad. She pointed to the index card fastened to the front of the kennel. "Says her name is Tinker. Some woman dropped her off."

"Huh," Winnie said, looking at the card. She shrugged. "I think she wants to be called Precious. Can you change the name?"

Irma smiled and wrote it down. "You bet." Then she knelt down in front of the chihuahua's kennel and made a kissing noise. "Precious?"

The little dog lifted her head. Winnie saw her two white ears spike at the sound of the name. The dog's big round eyes looked from Irma over to Winnie.

"Precious it is," Irma said with a smile.

Winnie couldn't be certain, but she thought the dog might be shivering a little less.

"This boy," Winnie said, approaching the fluffy white dog. "Guppy."

"Guppy?" Irma shook her head with a smile and wrote it down.

Winnie saw the name on the index card: Wolfy.

Nope, Guppy was a far more fitting name.

"Why is he here?" Winnie asked Irma.

"Stray. Found out in the desert. Don't let that thick coat fool you. It was a matted mess, and this guy was practically starving."

"How long has he been here?"

Irma consulted the index card. "A few weeks."

"Someone will take him this weekend," Winnie said. "I promise."

The dog gave a short bark and turned a circle in his kennel.

"Do you think he understood you?" Irma asked.

"I think he did," Winnie said.

Then she came to a kennel with a dog cowering in the corner. She looked bony. Her thin brown coat was bare in a few places. She kept her nose tucked down against her chest. She seemed to be trying to make herself as small as possible.

Winnie saw a boot. A fist. A rope yanked around the dog's neck.

She quickly shut off the image stream. She couldn't bear it.

"This one needs another dog in the family to show her how to be. She's had a very hard time. She needs a lot of patience and love."

Irma read the index card. She pointed to the given name. Winnie shook her head.

"Lolly," she said, because the name popped into her mind. Irma wrote it down.

Before coming here, Winnie wouldn't have thought she should rename any of the dogs. But now for some of them it seemed exactly right.

Why should they start their new lives with kinder, better owners, and still have to respond to the names given them by their previous, unworthy humans?

Even the dogs like Guppy, formerly Wolfy, who had gotten their names from some well-meaning staff person at the Center, should be allowed to start fresh with whatever name Winnie could sense suited them better.

And maybe some of the animals wanted to name themselves. Like the chihuahua who wanted to be called Precious.

Winnie continued her slow return down the rows of kennels, and then she heard the phrase again.

No one wants me.

She paused in front of the wire enclosure where a blocky-headed tan dog lay with his nose on top of his paws. He looked like a pit bull mix of some sort. Maybe even part Lab, by the look of his thick tail.

Winnie waited for him to make eye contact, but he stared listlessly at his kennel wall.

"Hit by a car," Irma said. "At least the driver took him to an emergency vet and even paid for it. But then he didn't know what else to do. No tag, no microchip. So he brought him here."

Winnie looked at the name some staff person had given him. *Charlie.* That sounded all right to her.

"Char-lie," Winnie called in a soft, sing-song voice. The dog continued to lie motionless on the bare concrete. His towel lay crumpled in a corner.

What do you need? she asked him inside her mind.

No one wants me, he said again.

Winnie crouched in front of the kennel and curled her fingers around the wire.

Charlie, look at me. Why would you say that?

He shifted his eyes in her direction. But his chin still lay on his paws.

Winnie wasn't sure what else to do. This wasn't her specialty. What would Chandra, the pet communicator, do in her place?

Do you like the name Charlie? Someone here thought it was a good name for you. But you can choose any name you want.

Again the dog's eyes shifted to Winnie. Then he stared again at his kennel wall.

The door at the end of the hallway opened. Four people entered, three women and one man, all of them carrying leashes. Two of the women looked middle-aged. One of the women and the man seemed to be in their late twenties.

"Walkies!" the man called out, and the barking rose to an excited pitch. Winnie covered her ears with her hands.

"These are some of our volunteers," Irma told her as she turned aside to make room for them to pass.

Winnie gave them a quick glance, but then returned her attention to Charlie.

As the commotion rose around them, Charlie remained silent, but slightly lifted his head. One of his eyebrows creased upward into his smooth forehead. He warily watched the volunteers.

"Should we go to the next room?" Irma shouted over the excited barks.

It sounded reasonable, yet some instinct told Winnie to wait.

Her legs were cramping, but she remained crouched in front of Charlie's kennel. She continued to study the dog's behavior.

The two older women had already latched their

leashes to two of the dogs and escorted them out of the room.

"They all get taken out to the exercise area twice a day," Irma said. "We're so lucky with our volunteers."

The younger woman smiled and gave Irma a little curtsy.

She was dressed like the other dog walkers, in jeans and an Animal Adoption Center T-shirt. She had curly black hair she wore back in a ponytail.

Charlie didn't like her. Winnie could feel it coming off him in waves. He wasn't afraid of her, but he didn't want her near.

The woman said, "Excuse me," and made a move toward opening Charlie's kennel.

Winnie creaked herself to standing and held out her hand for the leash.

"I'd like to walk him," Winnie said.

The young woman seemed surprised. She looked to Irma for direction.

"I don't think that's a good idea," the young woman said.

"It's all right, Crystal. Would you go get another leash? You can take out one of the others instead."

Crystal hesitated, but then she handed Winnie the leash. She smiled as though it wasn't a problem.

But Winnie could feel the woman's tension. She could see it in her eyes.

"Be careful," Crystal told her. "He's kind of a ... jerk."

Winnie could tell that Crystal wanted to call Charlie something else, but had modified it for the white-haired lady's benefit.

"He seems sweet to me," Winnie said.

Crystal shrugged. "He's gonna be hard to place. Just saying."

"Please don't say that in front of the dogs," Winnie snapped. She was surprised at the strength of her reaction, but she could feel her blood pressure start to rise.

Crystal wrinkled her eyebrows. She looked to Irma.

"She's right," Irma said in a friendly enough voice. "Now go ahead and get another leash. You have dogs waiting. They'd love to be walked!"

As soon as Crystal left the room, Winnie and Irma were alone again with the dogs.

"We have a hard time keeping volunteers," Irma said. "This work can be ... depressing."

"That one can go," Winnie told her. "She isn't good for the dogs. Is she, Charlie?"

The dog had his head up now and was looking at Winnie.

"Do you really think they can understand?" Irma asked. "I mean, I know what Mrs. Bristol said about you, but..." She twisted her rough hands together at her waist. "Tell me the truth. Because if I need to retrain everyone..."

"I think it's like surgery," Winnie said. "For years doctors and nurses said whatever they wanted about their patients during operations. They thought the patients couldn't hear them while they were under anesthetic.

"But then enough patients started reporting what they heard the surgeons say. They got it right, word for word. Now it's just accepted that everyone in the operating room should be careful what they say. Patients hear and they remember."

Irma thought about it. The door opened again and the male volunteer came for the next dog in line.

"Thanks, Chad," Irma told him. He smiled and continued his work.

As soon as they were alone again, Irma said, "You know, I've been worried about Charlie. After he came here, we kept him in the sick bay for several weeks until his leg healed. It's not that different from here—lots of dogs and cats in rows of kennels. But he always seemed so happy—even goofy. It's just that, ever since we brought him in here, he's seemed so depressed. I thought it was because he was missing his friends back in sick bay, but..."

"Does Crystal volunteer in the sick bay?"

"No. In fact, she just started a few weeks ago."

Winnie gave her a significant look.

"Okay, I understand. Either retraining, or she has to go."

A different kind of thought popped into Winnie's mind. "You have money now. Can't you hire more staff?"

"We're trying to build on to this place," Irma said. "Give all the animals more room. Penny did leave us a lot of money, but it still only goes so far. At some point the executor of her estate will sell her house, too, and then we'll get more then. But I wouldn't want to hurry little King Arthur along. Such a sweet dog."

Winnie felt an unexpected pain in the center of her chest.

She pressed her hand there, then tried to rub the pain away.

"Are you all right?" Irma asked.

"Hm." Winnie nodded, but she couldn't dismiss the stab she had just felt in her heart.

She wasn't worried about her health. She wasn't having a heart attack. She had felt pains like this before. Someone was trying to get her attention.

She looked into Charlie's kennel. He was sitting up on his haunches now and watching Winnie.

Had the pain come from him?

I'll take care of you, Charlie, Winnie told him with her mind.

The dog tilted his big blocky head and gave her a slight wag of his tail.

We'll find you a good home. Someone does want you. They just haven't met you yet. You're a sweet and lovely boy. Someone will be lucky to have you.

The dog groaned the way Clover sometimes did, in a way Winnie interpreted as a deep sigh. Charlie seemed to relax as he laid his chin back down on his paws.

One room, and already a few dogs Winnie felt she could help. First by renaming Precious, Guppy, and Lolly, and second by making sure Crystal didn't work with Charlie anymore.

She would do what she could with as many animals as possible before the weekend, but right now she felt especially committed to finding the right match for Charlie. It had to be someone who would love and appreciate this sensitive boy.

Winnie glanced at her watch. It was past noon.

If all the rooms were going to be like this one, she needed to eat and keep up her strength.

And then came that pain again just to the right of her heart.

She laid her hand flat over it.

Was one of the other animals calling to her right now, begging her to come and help?

She had been right to understand how daunting this experience would be.

But she had the skills to help in ways no one else here did.

And then she saw the image flash into her mind.

Suddenly Winnie knew exactly who was reaching out.

4

F
ebruary days were short. It was already dusk by
the time Winnie left the Animal Adoption Center.

She was bushed. Her mind felt fatigued. Her legs felt cramped from all the hours crouching in front of the kennels of dogs who needed her special attention.

Clover needed her dinner. Winnie needed hers, too.

And she needed to spend some time strategizing. Because there was another piece of work that was obviously hers to do.

Clover greeted her at the door, leading with her nose.

"Oh, I know. Where have I been?" Winnie said. "Who are all these dogs?"

She let Clover sniff her pants as thoroughly as she wanted.

But the dog would have to follow her around the kitchen while she did it. Winnie needed bread. Two thick slices of the loaf she made yesterday, toasted. A bowl of leftover Hungarian mushroom soup. A whole bottle of fizzy water.

Clover finally gave up interest in Winnie's pants, in exchange for a full bowl of turkey-flavored kibble.

While her soup was reheating, Winnie sat on the couch and replenished her strength the best way she knew how, with an immediate dose of homemade chocolate chip cookies she kept on hand for emergencies just like this.

As the sugar rushed into her blood stream, Winnie closed her eyes and leaned her head back onto the cushions.

This might be tricky. Liars lied to the very end.

Clover finished inhaling her dinner and jumped up to join Winnie on the couch.

"What a day," Winnie told her. "But you know what? Your secret is out. I know you can talk to me now."

Clover opened her mouth and panted. Her tongue hung out comfortably between her teeth.

"I met some of the saddest dogs I've ever seen," Winnie said. Clover thumped her tail. "But we'll find them families. Even if it takes months. So I might not be home as much as usual for a while."

If Clover understood, Winnie couldn't tell from the way she was behaving. The dog stood up on the couch, turned around once in a circle, and then lay back down closer to Winnie. Winnie patted the Lab's rump and ate another cookie.

After her warm and filling dinner of soup and buttered toast, Winnie felt renewed enough to pick up her cell phone and make a call.

"I need some legal advice," she told her lawyer niece Rose. Then Winnie explained the image she had seen while she stood inside the room of kennels at the Center.

"Be careful," Rose said. "Do you want me to come with you?"

"Irma will come," Winnie said. "I'll call you as soon as we're done."

She disconnected the call and sat inside her warm and cozy house. Clover snored beside her. Winnie knew that both she and the dog led a very good life.

But not all dogs had that same privilege. And while Winnie couldn't help all of the dogs in the world, she could at least help a few.

And right now, she needed a plan to help one little dog in particular.

She had a few ideas about how to rescue Mrs. Bristol's dog, King Arthur.

Winnie closed her eyes and spoke to him. She hoped that he could hear her.

I'm coming, King Arthur. I heard you today. I'll come save you as soon as I can.

5

Wednesday, Winnie's second day at the Animal Adoption Center, and just two days away from the Valentine's Weekend Adopt-a-thon.

Irma introduced Winnie to one of her wizards in the back offices.

"This is Nessa." A woman in her early thirties smiled over at Winnie from where she sat behind a computer. She had light brown hair pulled back into a ponytail. She wore one of the Center's sweatshirts, this one in light gray. Winnie could see the woman's bloodshot blue eyes looking out at her from behind her large round glasses.

"How long have you been here?" Irma asked her.

Nessa glanced at the clock. "Since seven. But I got

another thirty pictures entered." She made a fist into the air and croaked, "Woo-hoo!"

"Nessa writes up all the animal profiles for our website," Irma explained. "We got a little behind."

Nessa was back to typing. "*I* got a little behind," she said good-naturedly without looking up.

"A newborn will do that," Irma said. "Who's watching her?"

"My mom today, Dave tomorrow. He's taking off work so I can get this all done."

"Well, we won't keep you," Winnie said. She could feel the tension streaming off of the woman's shoulders.

"Hey," Nessa said as Winnie and Irma made for the door. "I like all the new names. They really suit them. I think some of them even look happier in their photos now."

Winnie hated to bother her, but now she was too curious to let it go. "Do you have Charlie yet?"

Nessa clicked a few keys and motioned for Winnie to come read the screen over her shoulder.

This was not the face Winnie had seen yesterday. "When did you take this?" she asked.

Irma looked, too. "In the sick bay about a month ago."

No wonder Irma had been worried about the change in his disposition. Charlie had gone from a wide, toothy grin to the somber dog Winnie saw in his kennel yesterday.

"Here's his buddy," Nessa said, clicking over to a different profile. Winnie saw an orange tabby kitten, overloaded with cuteness, reaching out her paws and staring with her big eyes into the camera.

"I'm hoping someone will take them together," Nessa said. "Wouldn't that be sweet? I think all the kittens in that litter have been cleared now for adoption."

"We don't require it, of course," Irma told Winnie, "but sometimes people are willing to take bonded pairs."

"That's always our favorite," Nessa said.

Winnie could understand why.

Two animals rescued in one adoption. She had a new focus for her work today.

She would ask the animals she spoke to whether they had a friend they hoped could go to the same home with them.

Winnie checked her watch. "We should get started."

This was going to be a somewhat shortened day.

Winnie had already made a few phone calls from the parking lot of the Center just after nine o'clock. The people she spoke to confirmed what she suspected.

So she made one more phone call, arranging for an appointment this afternoon.

Piece by piece, Winnie's plan was shifting into place within her mind.

But first she had animals to help here at the Center. Irma grabbed her notebook from the day before and found another pen, then she and Winnie stepped into one of the cat rooms.

Good morning! I'm Winnie. I'm here to help you all find good homes. Please tell me what kinds of things you like and don't like. Tell me if you have any special friends here. Then we'll try to match you with the perfect person.

The din was different from a roomful of barking dogs. The cats sounded more like a burbling stream compared to a roaring waterfall.

Winnie smiled inside her heart. She loved to use her gifts this way.

The kennels were stacked three high and then side by side to fill out the two rows. Winnie looked at the nametag on the first kennel: Scat.

He was an older black cat with a little divot taken out of his right ear. There were white patches on his front paws. The cat looked at Winnie with wide and curious yellow eyes. She poked her finger through the wires and Scat licked it with the delicate tip of his tongue.

The information popped into Winnie's mind. Suddenly she knew something about this cat.

"He hates that name," Winnie told Irma. "His last owner gave it to him." Irma raised her pen to her pad.

Winnie listened for a moment for a new name to pop just as easily into her head.

Instead Winnie saw an image of the black cat sleeping on top of a white upholstered chair. Sunlight streamed in through a window and warmed his silky back.

A kind-looking middle-aged woman sat on a chair beside him, reading a book. She reached over to stroke the cat's head. Winnie could feel how much he loved the woman's touch.

Winnie sensed this wasn't a scene from Scat's past. The cat inside the kennel looked too skinny and bedraggled to have come from a pampered life like that.

But as soon as she stopped trying to analyze the image, and allowed herself simply to feel the emotions of the cat instead, Winnie understood. She looked into Scat's eyes and smiled.

The black cat had obviously listened to what Winnie said when she first entered the room. *Tell me what kinds of things you like and don't like.*

The black cat was sending Winnie a wish.

She kept her index finger curled around the wire of his cage. He licked her knuckle again.

"You need a better name," she told him. "Something fun and sweet to go with your new life. And maybe something ... a little sassy." The name sprang into

Winnie's mind. "Boots." Because of his white paws. But then she heard the rest of it: "Boots McCoy."

It was the first time she had given any of the animals a surname. Boots McCoy seemed to approve. He answered with a loud and hearty meow.

Irma laughed and wrote down the new name.

Winnie could have spent the next hour talking with the cat, but she had to move on to all the others. Time was ticking away.

And King Arthur was very much on her mind.

Winnie sometimes thought of her clairvoyant ability as a flashlight she held inside a dark and vast warehouse. She couldn't just flip on a light and see everything at once. Instead her clairvoyance showed her whatever was focused within the limited beam.

Sometimes reading a word or a name made information suddenly pop into her mind. The same if she saw a photograph. She would receive information about that person or thing or place.

Standing in a room of dog kennels yesterday, Winnie had asked Irma if the Center could use some of Mrs. Bristol's bequest to hire more people for the staff.

"Penny did leave us a lot of money, but it still only goes so far. At some point the executor of her estate will sell her house, too, and then we'll get more then. But I wouldn't want to hurry little King Arthur along. Such a sweet dog."

Then Winnie had felt a pain in her chest.

Because hearing the name King Arthur had clicked on her flashlight.

The beam of light swung around and located the little dog.

And what Winnie saw of him made her heart hurt.

Five or six years ago, when Winnie saw him riding on top of a little blue blanket on top of Penny Bristol's rolling walker, King Arthur was a handsome, well-groomed dog who, even though he was in pain from his misplaced rib, still looked healthy and well-fed.

In the image that flashed into Winnie's mind yesterday, King Arthur now looked skinny and sick, with goopy discharge coming from his eyes. He took long, wheezy breaths as though something were wrong with his lungs.

His coat looked dirty and matted. Obviously he wasn't being groomed every week by Pierre LeFranc, as specified within Mrs. Bristol's will.

That had been one of Winnie's calls this morning. Mr. LeFranc confirmed in an icy tone that he had been informed that his services were no longer required.

"Who fired you?" Winnie asked him.

"That Charlotte woman," he said.

Charlotte Amper, the dog's caretaker designated in Mrs. Bristol's will.

A second call confirmed that Margery, the cook who made all of the spaniel's favorite foods, had also been fired within the first week after Charlotte Amper took over the house.

"I don't know why," Margery said. "It's dumb. I was fully paid for. She could have had me cook for her the whole time she was there."

Winnie suspected the reason. "What happened to your salary once you left?"

"I assume it went back into the household expense account," said Margery. "Not that she needed it. Do you know how much was already there?"

She told Winnie the figure. It was even more than she had imagined.

"Why so much?" Winnie asked.

"Because Mrs. Bristol grew up poor," Margery said. "She told me how happy it made her never to have to worry anymore whether she could afford groceries or gas or anything else that was so hard for her parents to buy. She didn't even mind going to the dentist, because her father told her only rich people could afford good teeth."

Winnie admired Mrs. Bristol even more for leaving most of her wealth to a charity that took care of animals.

Last night, Winnie's niece Rose confirmed that if someone wasn't abiding by the terms of a will, the executor of the estate could remove their right to receive anything further.

And if someone defrauded the estate by taking

money and goods that weren't theirs to have, then the estate could sue, and there might even be criminal liability for theft.

But Winnie hoped it wouldn't come to that.

She had a different plan in mind.

At noon she ate the peanut butter and strawberry jam sandwich she had packed for herself this morning. Then she and Irma continued visiting as many of the animals as they could before Winnie's watch alarm reminded her it was time to leave.

"We might not be back before close," Irma told the purple-haired receptionist, Kirsten.

Irma had changed into a clean Animal Adoption Center sweatshirt, and had given Winnie one to wear, too.

They drove in Irma's dusty, dinged-up Toyota 4Runner, since it had the Center's logo on the side.

Winnie wanted to look as official as possible.

Irma drove north for forty minutes, eventually coming to the wealthy subdivisions in the Catalina foothills. She had been to Penny Bristol's house before. She described it to Winnie on the way.

Mrs. Bristol's husband, Robert, had earned his fortune from inventing some manufacturing process Irma didn't know much about. He and Penny had traveled all around the world and had collected exotic furniture and art from the places where they went.

"Their house is like a museum," Irma said. "Very beautiful and tasteful. I could tell Penny was really proud of the things she and Robert collected."

As they pulled into the paved driveway in front of the large and elegant two-story house, Winnie said, "It's better if we don't say too much. Silence makes people nervous. They want to talk just to fill in the gaps. So we'll tell her why we're here, and then wait for her to explain."

Winnie checked her watch again. It was a little before four o'clock. Her appointment was in a half hour. She hoped she would be ready by then.

Irma rang the doorbell. Winnie could hear its musical notes chiming inside the house.

When a few minutes passed without any answer, Irma rang the bell again.

Winnie looked around at the front of the property. She remembered the will providing for landscaping, but most of the plants looked blackened from freezing, and only the various cacti had survived.

At last they heard some movement from inside the house.

Winnie reached over and pressed the doorbell again. She wanted to make sure Charlotte Amper felt properly annoyed.

"I'm coming!" a voice shouted.

Winnie smiled at Irma and pressed the doorbell again.

The door opened and Winnie had to adjust her line of sight by about half a foot lower than it was.

She expected to see someone her own height, but Charlotte Amper couldn't have been taller than five feet.

She added at least four more inches to her stature by wearing a tall, ratty wig with coils of black hair stacked on top of each other the way women in the 1800s might have worn it.

She looked like she might be in her late fifties, but the years had taken their toll. Her skin had a yellowish tint. Her eyes were only half open. Winnie could smell cigarette smoke on her wig and skin and clothes. And Charlotte Amper's breath reeked of alcohol.

She wore faded red sweatpants, bedroom slippers, and a T-shirt celebrating a steak house.

"Who are you?" Charlotte asked them.

"Remember me?" Irma asked, smiling. "I'm Irma Makelski from the Animal Adoption Center, and this is Dr. Parsons."

Winnie had told Irma to use her formal designation of doctor. It made a useful impression in a situation like this.

"Doctor?" Charlotte repeated.

"Yes," Winnie said. "We're here from the Center. Mrs. Bristol instructed us to make home visits every quarter."

Charlotte's eyes widened. She cursed under her breath.

"Hold on, hold on..." And she started closing the door.

"Oh no, Ms. Amper," Winnie said, pushing it back open. "Our instructions are to show up unannounced and see the condition of the house and Mrs. Bristol's dog exactly as they are."

Charlotte Amper's bottom lip sucked in and out while Winnie could see her brain frantically working.

She almost felt sorry for the woman, but the image of King Arthur still burned in her mind.

"Where is the dog?" Winnie asked.

Charlotte stared at her with wide open amber eyes.

Winnie waited. She took her own advice and did not try to fill the uncomfortable silence with words.

It took several long moments before Charlotte Amper repeated, "The dog..." She glanced behind her as if King Arthur might be right there underfoot.

Winnie surveyed the part of the room visible from the door. It did not look like a museum, the way Irma had described it. It looked like a frat house after a party.

There were bottles and cans and plates crusted with old food. The house smelled of cigarettes and garbage.

Charlotte Amper was a pig.

Winnie could see Irma scanning the room, too. It must be worse for her, having seen it in its former glory.

"Wasn't there a painting over there?" Irma asked, pointing.

Charlotte turned around and stayed in that position longer than seemed necessary.

"Yeah..." she finally said, and then she left it at that.

"The *dog*," Winnie said, more forcefully this time. This wasn't a game. She wasn't amused. King Arthur was somewhere in this house, suffering.

"I'll get him," Charlotte said, and she made some slight movement toward her left.

But Winnie suddenly felt a rising panic. She needed to see the dog *now*.

"Take us to him. This instant," Winnie said. She pushed into the house and glared at the woman who had so abused Penny Bristol's trust.

Charlotte looked from Winnie to Irma, as though trying to think of some angle that still might work, but then her shoulders sagged. She must have realized she was well and truly caught.

She led the two of them through what had once been a beautiful living room, then into the kitchen where the garbage was piled up even worse than Winnie expected.

She almost asked, "What is *wrong* with you?" But she knew what was wrong. She had studied psychology for enough years that she knew a disturbed mind when she saw it.

Again, she might have felt sorry for Charlotte Amper if the woman simply kept her destruction to herself. But she had preyed on Mrs. Bristol, promising her she would take care of King Arthur and this home.

Winnie hated liars. And she could never forgive anyone who would hurt a dog.

Charlotte continued leading them toward a door at the back of the house.

She opened it onto a laundry room.

King Arthur looked up from his dirty dog bed on the floor.

The small room had no windows. At least the light was on.

Irma knelt on the tile and spoke softly to the dog. King Arthur whimpered in response.

Despite the impression she wanted to give, Dr. Parsons was not a veterinarian. She let Irma examine the dog. Winnie stood in the doorway, while Charlotte Amper waited nervously outside.

Irma began describing all that was wrong. "These nails haven't been cut for three months. I'm sure he can barely walk. He has some kind of infection in his eyes and ears. And it sounds like he might have pneumonia."

Winnie could hear his wheezing breath, just as she heard it the day before.

The dog looked at Irma through his gunky eyes. He whimpered at her touch.

Irma picked up his bed, with King Arthur cradled inside. Winnie stepped out of the room and Irma carried the dog past Charlotte Amper.

"I can't even speak to you, I'm so angry," she told Charlotte with venom in her eyes.

And true to her word, Irma continued carrying the dog through the house and out the front door, presumably to settle him gently in the backseat of her car.

The doorbell rang, and Winnie knew it wasn't Irma.

She checked her watch. Right on time. She strode to the front door to receive her guest.

The young man wore blue cotton workpants and a shirt with his name over the pocket.

"Hello, Kyle," Winnie said. "I don't know how many doors there are. Go ahead and do whatever you need."

His van was parked in the driveway behind Irma's Toyota. The sign on the side said *A-Best Mobile Locksmith*.

"What's he here for?" Charlotte Amper demanded.

"He's changing the locks. You're moving out right now."

Charlotte's bottom lip sputtered in and out again. She grabbed her lofty wig and threw it to the ground. Her unhealthy habits had left her with gray, gristly hair. Although even that looked better than the wig.

"You can't do this!" Charlotte shouted, but Winnie calmly stared her down.

"Fraud is a crime. We've spoken to the estate's lawyer. You have bigger worries than where you're going to stay tonight."

Charlotte looked frantically around the living room. She reminded Winnie of someone realizing her house was on fire, and trying to decide in a split second what to save.

"Do you have clothes?" Winnie asked.

"'Course I have clothes!"

"Then let's go pack them. You only have an hour."

Irma came back into the house at a trot. She deliberately refused to look at Charlotte.

"I need to get him to the vet," Irma said. "I'm sure I'll have to leave him overnight. I'll come back and get you as soon as I can."

"Or I can call a taxi," Winnie said. "Don't worry about me. Please just make sure little Arthur is all right."

Then she felt a tug on her heart. She couldn't just let the dog leave. Winnie ran out after Irma.

King Arthur lay on his dirty bed in the backseat, wheezing with every breath.

Winnie stroked the dog's head. She leaned over and spoke to him softly.

"Thank you for telling me. You saved yourself. We'll take good care of you now, I promise."

She kissed his soft brown head between his long warm ears. Warm with an infection. Winnie recognized the smell of it from the few bouts of ear infection Clover had over the years.

But this one smelled much worse. She hoped the dog wouldn't lose his hearing as a result.

Winnie stroked her thumb across the little dog's forehead. Then she said goodbye and shut the door and let Irma drive him away.

Kyle the locksmith was still working on the front door. He had finished the knob and already moved on to the deadbolt.

Winnie drew in a breath of fresh air before plunging back into the filthy house. She knew by the time she got home tonight, her hair and clothes would smell of cigarettes.

She found Charlotte Amper upstairs in the master bedroom, messily throwing her clothes into a duffel bag.

For a moment Winnie considered searching the bag to make sure Charlotte hadn't stolen anything from the room.

There might be expensive jewelry in there. And probably mementos that had meant something to Mrs. Bristol.

But Charlotte had had total freedom inside this house for the past three months. Maybe she had already sold the painting in the living room that Irma thought was missing. She might have already stolen and sold Mrs. Bristol's jewelry, too. And who knew how many other items she might have taken that Mrs. Bristol trusted her to leave to be sold at some future time, with the proceeds all going to the Animal Adoption Center.

Winnie couldn't understand how a woman like Charlotte Amper ever gained Mrs. Bristol's trust. But like all con people, Charlotte must have put on a convincing act.

She probably dressed better and made sure she didn't stink of alcohol. She probably coddled the little dog, spoke baby talk to him—who knew. Mrs. Bristol must have seen something she liked in Charlotte Amper.

Winnie felt nothing but contempt for the con woman.

At times like these, Winnie had to fight some deep-seated urge to scold and lecture and to try to shame.

If someone like Charlotte Amper felt any shame right now, it was only because she had gotten caught. Somewhere in the forming of her character, she had missed the self-regulating chip that told her to stop before ever hurting people this way.

"This is mine," Charlotte said defensively as she grabbed a frilly robe off of its hanger.

Winnie doubted it was true, but she didn't care at the moment. She just wanted the Amper woman gone.

Charlotte Amper shoved a few more shirts into her

duffel, then she zipped it up and hauled it onto her stooped shoulder.

Winnie followed her down the stairs. Charlotte cast her gaze around the bottom floor. But with Winnie tailing her so closely, she must have decided that any further theft wasn't worth it.

She bullied her way past burly young Kyle, and she headed toward the garage.

Winnie continued following her. She was aware of the Cadillac that must be inside.

Charlotte looked back, no doubt to see if anyone was watching. She made a face at Winnie, then dug out a set of keys from the front pocket of her dirty, faded red sweatpants.

She punched in a code to the control pad at the side of the garage. The door quietly slid up, revealing the Cadillac and an old beater Chevy Celebrity in the space beside it.

Charlotte opened the back door of the Celebrity and threw her duffel on the seat. Then she got in and fired up the rough-sounding engine.

The car sputtered and belched out smoke from the tailpipe. But it worked, and Charlotte put in reverse.

She left the garage door up. Winnie didn't know the code to put it down. She hoped it was written someplace for someone to find—

And there. The four numbers flashed into Winnie's

mind. Her clairvoyant flashlight had found the keypad in that dark, vast warehouse.

Charlotte passed Winnie and made a rude gesture out of her window.

Winnie ignored her and went to close the garage door.

As she walked back to the house, Winnie started making a mental list of all the things she could do now to make everything better.

The estate had all the money it needed to hire cleaners and landscapers and appraisers and whatever else Mrs. Bristol's house and its contents might need.

But she came to a halt in front of Kyle's locksmith van, and realized she had no part to play anymore.

She was only a bystander in this twisted situation. This was for other people to fix.

Her work was back at the Animal Adoption Center right now. There were so many animals there she still needed to meet.

Her car was still there, too. But it was getting late. She needed to get home to feed Clover.

Winnie called Irma's cell phone, but it went straight to voicemail. She must not have it on while she was at the vet.

Winnie left a message. "I'll take a cab home. Don't worry about me. And I'll take a cab to the Center in the morning. We'll just add it to my bill."

But then an image flashed into Winnie's mind.

She was sure Mrs. Bristol would approve.

"Actually," Winnie continued on Irma's voicemail, "I'll take Mrs. Bristol's car home. We can bring it back here tomorrow."

Winnie clicked off the call. She could see in her mind's eye exactly where the Cadillac keys were hanging on a hook inside the front door.

She found the keys, but now she was missing Kyle. She could hear him somewhere at the back of the house.

"I need to go," she told him. "Does someone have to be here while you work?"

"Nope, we're insured and I'm incredibly honest."

The young man grinned at Winnie, and she opened her vision to look at the young man's aura.

"Yes, I believe you are," she told him. She fished out her slim wallet from the pocket of her purple vest and pulled out two twenty dollar bills. Although the estate lawyer had told her that the estate would pay for the locksmith, Winnie wanted to tip him herself.

The Cadillac was relatively clean. Charlotte must not have driven it very much.

Winnie thought of the provision in Section 6 of Penny Bristol's will that would pay for gas so Charlotte Amper could drive King Arthur around to look at the foothills scenery.

That poor little dog. Winnie could only hope he would be all right.

As for the liar and thief Charlotte Amper, Winnie would leave it to the estate's lawyer to decide what to do.

Winnie started up the Cadillac and checked the gas gauge. There was still half a tank. More than enough to get home.

The sun had already set by the time she arrived home. Once again Clover sniffed her clothes and gave Winnie a thorough inspection.

Winnie could smell the cigarette smoke on her clothes. She gave Clover her dinner, then undressed and took a long shower.

By the time she got out, there was a message on her phone. Irma had called with an update on King Arthur.

She had been right about the infections in his eyes and ears, and right that he had pneumonia.

The vet was keeping him overnight to give him antibiotics and liquids in an IV. The dog was seriously malnourished and dehydrated.

As Winnie listened to the list of ailments, she could feel her skin getting warmer as the anger inside her rose.

But she had learned long ago that anger did not motivate her, it only drained her. So she concentrated on letting the red rage subside.

Her gift had allowed her to hear King Arthur's plea.

That was what mattered now. Winnie was grateful she could help a poor dog in need. That should be her focus.

But she spared a thought for where Charlotte Amper was now. And her mind provided the answer.

Winnie saw the woman in a dark, dingy house, smoking and drinking from a tall can of beer.

This must be where she lived when she met Penny Bristol. She had to have lived somewhere.

So now she would simply resume her former life.

And maybe look for the next person she could fool into thinking she was trustworthy and would take good care of their dog after the person was gone.

Winnie shook her head to clear it. She didn't want to know any more about that Amper woman.

Instead, she sent out a loving thought to King Arthur.

Sleep well, and I'll see you tomorrow.

As busy as she knew she would be at the Center, Winnie knew she would also need to see King Arthur. The little dog had wedged himself like a sliver inside Winnie's heart. She needed to see him happy and well again.

It was probably too soon to think of him being placed with a loving family at the Valentine's Adopt-a-thon, but Winnie knew that Irma would find him a good home when it was time.

Winnie reheated some of the lasagna she had made over the weekend. Then she sat with Clover on the couch and reflected on the day.

The dog scooted closer to Winnie, then laid her head on Winnie's lap. It was exactly what Winnie needed.

Some night soon King Arthur would be sitting with someone just like this. Winnie could picture it in her mind. His eyes were clear, he had been bathed and brushed, and his ribs no longer showed through his coat.

A hand stroked softly down the little dog's side. He sighed and settled in closer.

There was another dog's nose sharing the person's lap from the other side.

How sweet. King Arthur would have a brother or sister.

But then the image shifted upward, and showed Winnie the whole room.

"No," she said, with a laugh of surprise. But it was too late to deny it, she had already seen this glimpse of the future.

Her visions didn't lie. But Winnie knew that the future was never set. People had free will. The future was always malleable.

But did Winnie want to change this particular future? Now that she had seen how it could be?

Winnie sitting in the center of her couch, Clover on one side, sweet little King Arthur on the other.

Winnie still wasn't certain that she and Clover could communicate this way, but she experimented anyway by forwarding the image to Clover's mind.

"What do you think?" Winnie asked her out loud. "Do you want a little brother? Actually, he's probably older than you. But he is smaller."

Whether it was from the sound of Winnie's voice or because Clover actually knew what Winnie was saying, the Labrador thumped her tail.

"You should meet him first. See if you like him," Winnie said. Clover thumped her tail again.

She could resist this future, but why would she want to? Maybe Clover had been wishing she had a friend.

Winnie returned Irma's call. Irma sounded tired, but she seemed upbeat about King Arthur's recovery.

"I think I have a new home for him," Winnie said.

"You do? That's great!"

Winnie told her the happy news.

"It's too perfect," Irma said. "Do you know how happy Penny would be? She would love to know that you were taking care of her dog for the rest of his life."

Winnie could feel it, too. A comforting warmth inside her chest.

She had no doubt that Penny Bristol would approve.

Before Irma let her go, she wanted Winnie to give

her all the nitty-gritty details about the eviction of Charlotte Amper.

Winnie found she could tell it now without feeling any rage.

Because although King Arthur had to endure three terrible months, in the end, everything had come out all right.

Irma yawned. "I'm beat. I want to be at the Center early tomorrow. See you in the morning."

"I'll be there," Winnie promised.

Then she sat on the couch with Clover and thought about Mrs. Bristol's little dog.

Winnie sometimes wondered if people understood the magic in their own lives.

The cause and effect. How their good deeds could lead to good in return.

And how despite the way it sometimes seemed in the short run, in the long run the universe seemed to tilt in favor of eventually letting the good guys win.

Penny Bristol was generous and kind. She left her wealth to help homeless animals.

She left a separate fund for the Animal Adoption Center to hire Winnie Parsons.

While Winnie was helping them, she saw a vision of King Arthur.

Some might say that Winnie and Irma saved Penny

Bristol's dog. But it was really Mrs. Bristol's kindness and generosity that saved her dog.

Winnie could draw the step-by-step diagram in her mind. Irma was right, it was actually perfect.

And along that same path, Winnie had met the animals at the shelter. And she would continue working hard to help all of them find new homes.

"It's too much," Winnie told Clover. "Too much!" She kissed Clover's soft yellow head.

She had to put herself to bed so she could get up early, too. Tomorrow was Thursday. She had so many animals still to meet before the Adopt-a-thon on Friday.

But as she settled between her flannel sheets, and Clover hopped up to claim her spot at the foot of the bed, Winnie could picture the little spaniel who would fit nicely on her other side.

In the morning, Winnie drove the Cadillac to the Center. She rushed in ready to start the day.

"Come on," Irma told her, taking Winnie by the arm. "Nessa has something to tell you."

Nessa still looked tired, either because of her newborn or because she had already been at her computer for hours, or more probably both.

But she let out a yip when she saw Winnie standing in her doorway. Nessa motioned excitedly for her to come look at the computer screen.

"Yesterday," Nessa said. "After you and Irma left." Then she leaned back in her chair and held out her hands to the screen like she was serving it to Winnie on a platter.

Charlie's photo was there, with his happy, grinning face. Next to it was the photo of an orange tabby kitten.

"Both of them," Nessa said. "Adopted together! A family with two kids came and took them right out of here."

"But how did they—" Winnie started to ask.

"They saw them on the website," Irma said. "Nessa's brilliant work."

Nessa blew on her fingernails and buffed them against her chest, a well-earned gesture of pride.

Winnie thought of the sad dog she had met just two days ago.

No one wants me.

She had promised him he would find his family, and that promise came true.

And to have his little kitten friend along. It was too sweet and wonderful for words.

"Okay, let's go," Winnie told Irma. Now that she had a taste of the thrill of seeing two of these animals adopted, she wanted to help get every single one of them find a new home.

She had refined her techniques over the past two days. Her interviews flowed faster and more smoothly.

By the end of Thursday afternoon, she had visited all of the dogs and cats.

There were still the birds, and a few ferrets, and an iguana, and other assorted pets. She would have to get to them on Monday.

Although the Valentine's Weekend Adopt-a-thon was the Center's big event, Charlie and his kitten friend had proven that people would look for pets on the website, too.

And more animals would keep coming in, because that was the nature of shelters. Winnie would still be needed, and she was happy to help.

But for now she just wanted to get back in her own car and drive to the vet's office before it closed.

King Arthur had responded well to the antibiotics and hydration. If Winnie wanted to, she could take him home tonight.

He would still need medication and extra care for a few more weeks, but the veterinarian thought the danger was over.

They had bathed him there, and clipped his overgrown toenails, and someone had brushed out his fur. He didn't look as dapper as he did when Winnie first met him, but at least he was clean again.

They brought him out to the lobby, and she bent down and scooped King Arthur into her arms.

"Do you want to come home with me?" Winnie asked him.

The dog's eyes were clear now, not gooped with infection.

King Arthur looked into Winnie's eyes and his tongue came out and he happily panted.

She was used to Clover's thick Labrador tail swishing against Winnie's leg or thumping on the furniture.

But King Arthur's smaller tail would do just as well, and it told Winnie everything she needed to know.

It wagged against her arm as the dog panted and lightly wheezed. Winnie could feel the dog's heart beating against his ribs.

One of those ribs had slipped out of place before, leading Penny Bristol to bring her dog—of all places—to the parapsychology lab.

Winnie had been the one to help her. And now here was Winnie again.

Holding the little spaniel in her arms. Hugging him close to her heart.

Penny Bristol was magic, and she never knew it.

But Winnie hoped that somehow Penny Bristol knew it now.

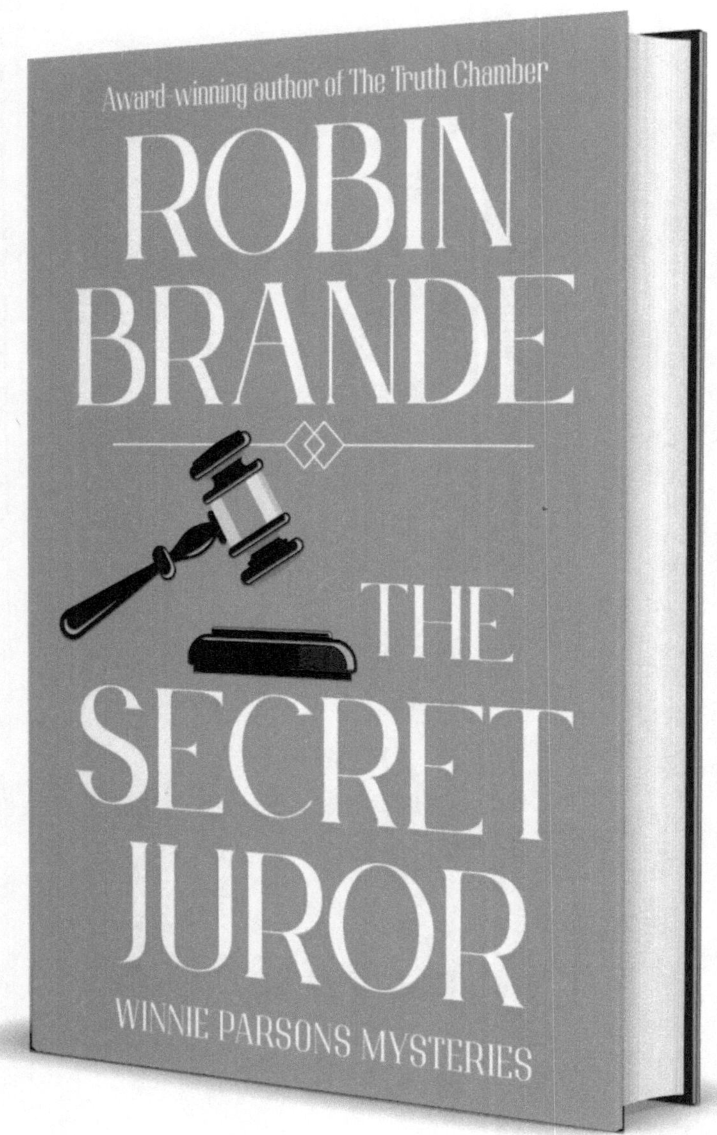

Liars can't hide
from Winnie Parsons.
But they sure keep trying.

The mind is a mysterious place. And the truth can change your life.

Stories of life after death,
miracle healings,
communication with
other species, and more.

Stories of life after death, second chances, and enduring love.

ABOUT THE AUTHOR

Robin Brande is an award-winning author, former trial attorney, black belt in martial arts, wilderness medic, and Reiki Master.

She writes in multiple genres, including mystery, fantasy, science fiction, young adult, romance, and self-help. She is also a designer and maker whose work celebrates the bookish life.

For more information:
robinbrande.com